ntroduction

Soul Songs is the story of a singer-songwriter with the unique gift of spontaneous composition. He, Immanuel, is able to spontaneously sing the song of a misplaced stranger's soul, tell him who he really is, and set him back on the path of his personal purpose all within seconds of meeting him.

However, Immanuel is unable to sing his own soul song because he was adopted at birth and does not know anything about his heritage or who he is. This void in his life leads to other problems in his music career, love relationships, and ability to sustain any type of professional activity. It also leads him to entertain dark, destructive behaviors that he cannot gain mastery over.

In the course of Immanuel's sojourn, he meets a woman who falls in love with him. He also falls in love but his emotions are twisted by his struggles. So he cannot express love in reciprocity; instead he tools around with seduction and rejection to meet his aims.

In the course of their relationship, she, Aimee, discovers that they truly are soul mates, and in her research career she actually discovers the creation of a new soul. Thus the story continues into profound and unknown territory reaching a marvelous conclusion.

1

Soul Songs is a Novella, a small novel written in the brisk style most easily convertible to screenplay for film. The reason for this is because of the colorful elements inherent in the story which would convert most artfully to screen for visual media representation.

As such there is less narration and the action is largely driven by the dialogue. Much is left to the imagination and visualization of the reader in order to personalize the story rather than to be confined to the writer's exposition. Also being a highly poetic work, much is expressed in metaphor, innuendo, entendre, and poetic verse reaching to a greater level of depth, curiosity of mystery, and height of inspiration.

The complexly interwoven plotline gradually emerges and increases intensity through the literary exchanges of the main characters, as well as through their thoughts, actions, choices, and inclinations. The scientific content is partly new science and partly Sci-Fi. There are also Romance, Fantasy, Mystery, and Adventure elements. The characters in this story have been derived from real people, and the story itself is based upon a real love affair between two people who are similar to those portrayed in the rendering.

This genre-fusion story has been written for release in six versions: (1) Paperback printed book (2) E-book (3) E-book with imbedded music videos (4) Audio book (5) Music CDs (6) Feature film.

Soul Songs

An Original Story

by

Sevi Regis

Montford Regis of CGGS, Inc.

New York

One

Lunch hour plays at allegro in New York City. The percussion of people rushing around on crowded, chaotic streets resounds the unmistakable beat of the City. But this hectic pace forces people's souls into a frozen state where they become numb and detached from the big picture of life's purpose and meaning. Hustling about, barely able to breathe from all the burdens placed on them, they play, like robots, cogs in the grinding wheel.

And so it is... the mission of the artist, to grab hold of the harried masses and stop time long enough for a vital connection to be made with a reminder of what this is all about: you're not a machine, an odd mutation of cells, a faceless number, a pawn on some grand chessboard! You are a unique, living soul who has a specific purpose and meaningful expression to deposit into this vast, uncertain sea of bittersweet dreams...

Artists Aimee Lucina and Clara Brightwater stop for lunch at the busy Crosstown Café. A corner table is being cleared; it has enough space to rest the framed paintings they've been carrying. They walk over and sit down.

Clara: "For the next show I think we should paint a series together."

Aimee: "For sure! I want to translate my music to canvas. Would you be into that?"

Clara: "I don't know, sounds interesting..., but hasn't anyone tried that yet?"

Aimee: "Not the precise correlation between visible and audible tones... like just what is the color of A440? ... or middle C?"

Clara: "Huh... I like it! Such a cool concept... there's probably so much more to it..."

Aimee: "Definitely!"

Clara: "It's worth exploring... Never know what else we might find..."

Aimee and Clara venture down the hallowed hall where artists, musicians, philosophers, scientists, and theologians meet in peaceful wonder: a gallery of endless expression. All these definitive languages are translatable into each other, like a superstring theory of communication, the substance of synesthesia!

Aimee: "I'm basing my insights on the fact that the visible spectrum, as expressed by the rainbow reveals itself in seven distinct colors just as a musical scale contains seven notes."

Aimee continues to explain that the distance between each color, say from yellow to green, is an infinite journey, as is the distance between two notes, like in C to D, or even between two numbers, 1 to 2. Every minute incremental step in between is infinite and eternally approaches but barely ever reaches...

Clara: "Wow, you're right! I never thought of matching tone to tone..."

Aimee: "I've been researching this for a year, but I haven't been able to find which note accurately represents 'red' to begin the progression and identify the spectral sequence."

Clara: "How do they determine the relative comparability of each frequency?"

Aimee: "By the mathematical positioning of all that exists and their relative alignment with each other."

Clara: "Awesome! I don't know if I ever told you that sometimes, when I compose on the piano, I see ribbons of color shooting out of the music..."

Aimee: "Really? Me too! They say it's a rare ability... Another thing I discovered is that the primary colors: red, yellow, and blue correspond perfectly to a 1-3-5 chord. And the perfect complement of red is green, which would be the 4th chord in a key, like in the key of G, the C chord leading to the D. And we know in design, these colors are most harmonious."

Clara: "Yeah, but they say: 'silence is golden' so maybe sometimes it's not only what you hear and see… but also what you don't hear and see that has the strongest impact. Ha!"

Aimee: "So true! Every cell in the body tunes itself to the music around it, like life imitating art."

Clara: "What inspires more creativity than the body and soul? Art imitating life! But you're right; it's amazing how a song sounds when you transpose it from a major key to a minor; changes the emotional vibe, happy to sad instantly with the halftone drop."

Aimee: "That has spiritual implications too. Dropping the major 3rd to a minor 3rd is reflected in ancient folk and liturgical music. Most of what was composed prior to the first Century AD appears to have been written in minor keys."

They continue to discuss recent brain scan studies evidencing the different genres of music and their specific effects on neurochemistry and synaptic transmission, as well as new research in plant studies. This research has demonstrated that music influences the hormonal and biochemical milieu of the listener. One type of music causes a certain effect, and so on...

A few blocks away..., a minstrel wearing a V-neck black velvet shirt and jeans strolls the streets through the hurried crowd, a sandwich in hand, his guitar strapped to his back. His phone rings; he looks at the number dialing in, but ignores it.

He passes a war veteran pleading for money, shaking his cup at passersby. Since no one gives the beggar anything, Immanuel hands him the rest of his lunch. Ernest continues calling out to the preoccupied people hastily traversing the streets.

Ernest: "Thanks man! Ever been hungry? Every bite helps, Man!"

Immanuel passes him, but turns around to watch, as a couple of cops come and briskly usher Ernest along. Police Officer Vecchio prods him along with his nightstick.

Police Officer Vecchio: "You're blocking traffic! Let's go!"

Police Officer Vega: "Come on, you gotta move...! NOW!"

Ernest: "Sheeple..., check it out! If this is how they treat their warriors..., what's gonna happen to you?!"

Ernest reluctantly gathers his tattered baggage and hobbles around the side street corner. The cops watch until he's moved off the avenue, then they walk onward.

Meanwhile, Aimee and Clara finish their lunch discussion, pick up their artwork, and leave the Café. Aimee walks back to her studio loft; Clara heads across town.

Intuitively curious, Immanuel follows Ernest who resumes begging.

Only a few moments into his relocation, a rogue thief comes, pummels, and robs Ernest. As the robber runs away, Immanuel chases him, wrestles him to the ground, and subdues him. He holds the thief in a choke hold and wraps his legs around his waist, strangling him.

Immanuel: "You get off by robbing the poor, fkn' dirt bag! See how you like it!"

Immanuel takes back Ernest's money and also takes the thief's possessions and gives it all to Ernest.

Ernest: "Awesome, Bro! I would've had your back if I wasn't a busted up sack of shit."

Immanuel's phone rings again, he looks to see who's calling, but ignores it.

Immanuel: "Broken maybe, but not buried! You still got a gig to play. Hear ye!"

Ernest: "Kick it!"

Immanuel positions his guitar and plays a soul healing song about Ernest's life, telling him who he is, what his purpose is, and the intimate workings of his innermost dreams.

The spontaneous song title is: **"A Brother In Ernest:"**

Aimee had returned to her art studio, and is carefully framing several canvases for exhibit, when her publicist, Roger Falcone, working at his computer doing promotions, calls her with updates.

Aimee: "Hey, Roger…"

Roger: "Aimee, Dear, how are we doing? Is our collection ready for exhibit?"

Aimee: "Ah-ha! I'm framing the last one now."

Roger: "Good, 'cause I just posted the press release."

Aimee: "Stellar! Have I ever told you how amazing you are?"

Roger: "Not nearly enough…ha!"

Back on the street Immanuel finishes singing Ernest's soul song. The war veteran is amazed and deeply moved that someone recognizes him and cares enough to look deeper, beyond his circumstances.

Ernest: "Dude! You ID'd me! Totally rocked my soul! How'd you do that?"

Immanuel: "It's a gift I have."

Ernest: "Man..., that's some sick gift! Really, it's an awesome power! Where'd you get it?"

Immanuel looks at him and smiles, then packs up and walks away. Ernest gets excited and calls after him.

Ernest: "Hey Minstrel..., wait up! You're like some dusty, old Renaissance troubador with that velvet shirt and everything..., come on, Man..., tell the truth..., that's your chick magnet, right? Dude, listen up..., you forgot to tell me your name... and how I can get hooked up with my song?"

The police officers return. They gesture to Ernest to gather up his stuff and move again, while Immanuel keeps walking away, disappearing into the crowd.

Two

The next day Immanuel walks along the upper West Side and goes into Central Park. He finds a Brazilian woman, Marisa, sitting on a bench crying. Seeing her sadness, he gently sits next to her, takes his guitar out of its bag, and plays her soul song. It's about her broken heart and failed relationships. He names the song after her, **"Marisa, Meu Amor,"** and it means: *'In the sea of bitterness, I found my love.'* He serenades her in her native language, Portuguese, and also in English.

Amazed, she gasps, exclaims, then cries:

Marisa: "How do you know my name... and everything about me? Before you came I was feeling so invisible..."

She sings the refrain with him. Then the song finishes, and he puts his guitar away, moves over, and rests his arm around her shoulder for comfort. She leans on him and peacefully smiles.

Across town Aimee carries groceries back to her studio. She sees couples, dogs, and others pass on the street. She feels a momentary pang of loneliness, but then continues on her way. Fumbling for her keys the bag tears, she drops her items and one breaks. No one notices or helps.

Immanuel leaves the park and walks down the Avenue of the Americas. He finds Bill, an executive who has just been fired from his job. He's rumpled, sitting on a fountain ledge outside his office building, feeling dejected with his career stuffed in a box. Bill sits staring at the pink slip in his hand. He gets angry, crumples it up, and throws it to the curb. It lands by Immanuel's feet; he bends down and picks it up.

Immanuel: "Humn..., pink slip..., you got sacked?"

Bill: "Uh-huh.., just another piece of company trash! Now what?"

Immanuel: "You're not alone, Man..., I hear you!" Immanuel plays a song for discarded worker: **"Man On A Mission."**

After the song, Bill looks at Immanuel with restored dignity and fresh inspiration. Immanuel looks back while walking away...

Bill: "You know, I put my whole life into this dead end job and finished up with nothing. They fired me before my pension kicked in! You really think I've got some kind of purpose beyond this? Seriously?"

Immanuel: "Damn right! Don't you?"

14

Three

Later that evening at Aimee Lucina's lab, the cleaning crew works around experiments, apparatus, and the animal cages. Dr. Dalisay Corazon, Aimee's research associate, is working on one of their projects as the maintenance staff gets a little reckless.

Dalisay: "Please, be careful near the animals; Dr. Lucina considers them her pets."

Downtown, Immanuel walks by the Gallery where Aimee's exhibiting her current art series. She's playing and singing with Clara. He sees her from the outside, and feels curiously attracted. He comes in, looks around, watches her play, **"Kaleidoscopes And Rainbows"** and sees her name on all the paintings. After Aimee's performance, he goes over to her.

Immanuel: "I don't say this often, but, I'm impressed!"

Aimee: "Cool. Thanks! Glad you enjoyed the evening."

Immanuel: "I have indeed, and the night is young!"

Immanuel's cellphone rings; he looks to see who's calling, but ignores it. Then he walks over and picks up her guitar, caresses it in a sensuous way, and rubs it on his body.

On the opposite side of the gallery, Roger promotes Aimee's art to guests and the media.

Art Reporter: "This body of work is most unusual. It appears to have a visionary quality..."

Roger: "Oh, yes..., her style is very unique..., aha, visionary!"

Art Buyer: "I look at lots of art, but rarely find such dimensionality, and her colors..., pure whimsy!"

Roger: "Absolutely...! Aimee is delightfully whimsical, yet never at the expense of technique!"

Across the gallery, Immanuel continues his seduction of Aimee.

Immanuel: "Sexy curves and sultry tones, suits you! May I strum her?"

Aimee: "Sure, you play?"

Aimee listens, captured by his charisma, as he plays her soul song, **"Pleasing Princess Polymath."**

She looks at him with deep curiosity, and utters with wide open eyes, breathily, "Oh..., SIGH!" He smiles in response, turns his head away, and says, " Yeah!"

At Dr. Lucina's Lab, research associates work on their experiments as the cleaning crew repositions things. Dalisay tries to help by moving units that prove unstable. She fumbles and stumbles, calls out for help. Dr. Robert Takatis replies with an annoyed, controlling, condescending attitude before assisting.

Dalisay: "Whoo-hoo..., Robert..., night shift emergency!"

Robert: "Brainiac! How many times must I advise you, Dr. Corazon, don't attempt these things without my help!"

Meanwhile Roger is finishing up with the last guests as Aimee walks over to say goodnight to him. Immanuel fidgets in the corner until she returns to go for coffee with him.

Immanuel: "Down for a steamy midnight Java?"

Aimee smiles, nods her head in acceptance, then asks Roger if it's OK to go.

Back at the Lab, while walking and working around the lab, he complains, then darts over quietly.

Robert: "I feel like I'm conducting research in a monastery; everything's so damn hush-hush and clandestine! What's the big secret? Why haven't you told me what you and Dr. Lucina are working on?"

Dalisay: "We're observing genome activity at the moment of conception. That's all I can say..."

Immanuel and Aimee walk to Café Cariocca. He radiates a charismatic charm hard to resist.

Immanuel: "So..., Princess Polymath..., as a damsel of the new dawn...,who's your master?"

Aimee: "Humn... truthfully? I'm a free spirit so I don't have one!"

Immanuel: "We all bow to somebody. I say it's the one who ravages you most in bed, binds you to itself like a nursing mother; the mate you can't escape or rip from your head, 'cause deep within, he's more you than any other...!"

As they walk along a distracted mature woman carrying bags is about to step off the curb and be hit by a car. Immanuel sees this, runs and saves her. She goes her way amazed, they continue their discussion as if nothing happened. Aimee is impressed, smiles.

Immanuel: "You must find science even more demanding than art. Big commitment, to find what?"

Aimee: "The creation of a living soul..."

He opens the door for her. Men sitting around the Cafe notice Aimee and smile in a flirtatious manner while eyeing her. Immanuel is surprised by the attention she's getting and acts possessive. The host seats them at a corner booth crowned by an amber chandelier. His phone rings; he looks at the number, but ignores it. Their talk turns giddy.

Immanuel: "Hah, you've got a taste for the cryptic! That's savage, Babe! Intrigues me ...!"

Aimee: "Cool..., but I don't even know your name... I imagine you have one...?"

Immanuel: "Yes..., a name and a guitar..., What more do I need?"

Aimee: "Hah, that depends... Who are you?"

Immanuel: "I am ... Immanuel Apollo.... Immanuel means: 'God is with us', and Apollo, was the god of music. He also ruled over the seven divine forces... But I don't believe any of that!"

Aimee: "Well..., it is all mythological..."

Immanuel: "Perhaps..., but can you imagine anyone that insanely powerful? Now that is way too much deity..., even for me!"

A brazen man passes their table, flirts openly with Aimee, making Immanuel annoyed and jealous. Out of retribution he flirts with the waitress who flirts back repeatedly, desperate for attention. The plain waitress is attracted to him, so she acts provocatively.

He plays sly head games with the Waitress who gets flustered, bangs into a busboy and drops her tray in nervous commotion.

Immanuel: "And you are: Aimee Lucina, which means?"

Aimee: "Aimee, as you correctly pronounce as: Ehm-may, means 'love', and Lucina means 'light-bearer'. And it is fitting, I do love the light of truth..."

Immanuel: "Yeah, but truth is relative and elusive. Falling for what you mistake to be true will only break your sweet heart!"

He stands up to pay and leave, reaching for Aimee's hand. The waitress runs over with the check, primps, flirts, and slips her number to him discreetly. He subtly shows it to Aimee, laughs, crumples it up, and throws it on the table like trash. But as he escorts Aimee ahead, he sneakily picks the crumpled phone number up again, and puts it in his pocket.

Some guys arguing outside, start shoving each other, ready to fight. He leaves her inside the cafe, goes out, makes peace, and returns to their discussion.

Immanuel: "Ha... you want truth? People are content in their bullshit! Besides, there's a lot of truth in myth, and a lot of myth about truth. It's been my experience, no one knows the difference or cares..."

As they walk to Aimee's residence together...

Aimee: "But truth is everything; nothing else is real..."

Immanuel: "Nah, it's all subjective, a matter of opinion. One man's truth is another man's fallacy. As soon as you think something is true, it defiantly exposes itself as false."

Aimee: "I know things can appear that way at times; but some things remain true forever, like love"

Immanuel: "Love? Ha! Naïve, but cute. Truth is about facts, even though when you finally find one, it disappears into another question?"

They pause in the misty quietude, as people walk their dogs and pass silently. In front of her building, he kisses her hand, she smiles coyly. Then he gets up close, intimate, and speaks in a soft, warm, deep tone.

Immanuel: "But I suppose, there's a thrill in the chase...!"

She smiles at him and puts her head down. He reaches out and caresses her hair.

Immanuel: "Your aura... it rests upon you like a crown... When may I behold it again?"

Four

The next day, Aimee and Dalisay are working on their research in the Lab. Robert eavesdrops trying to overhear their discussion. He moves around their work area and positions himself strategically to watch what they are doing on their electron microscopes. Aimee has just completed a routine procedure when she makes a startling discovery.

Aimee: "Wow! I just saw something weird..."

Dalisay stops what she's doing and goes over to look into the scope.

Dalisay: "That is strange! What do you think it is?"

Aimee: "Appears like a vibration of sorts..."

Dalisay: "Was this conducted as a standard in vitro fertilization...? Because I'm clueless!"

Aimee: "Yes..., it was... Let's increase the magnification and make this contrast pop..."

Dalisay: "It's still fuzzy; where's the lens cleaner?"

Aimee: "Yeah..., it's in my office. I'll get it."

Aimee leaves the research floor to get the lens cleaner from her office. Arriving, she finds Robert digging around in her files and on her computer. She stands in doorway observing, then confronts him.

Aimee: "What are you doing in here?"

Robert: "I'm conducting remedial research! Why..., you may ask? Because you forced me to... since you insist on being so blasted secretive!"

Aimee: "Excuse me! My study is incomplete, unpublished, and confidential!"

Robert slams her desk drawer, bangs the door on his way out, then faces off with her, before ranting his way up the hallway.

Robert: "Oh..., come now, Dr. Do-Gooder, science and its sacrosanct knowledge are for public consumption not to be hoarded by snickering egotists hungry for fame, fortune and fright nights of fraternal funnery while scheming to make a renowned name only for themselves! Now of all people..., you should know that!"

A little later, across town, Immanuel arrives at an early evening gig only to be turned away at the door by the Club Owner, Ben.

Ben: "Ticket and ID?"

Immanuel: "I don't need that; I'm the artist playing here tonight."

Ben: "Ah-ha..., I don't think so!"

Immanuel: "Dude, you're misinformed! Check your calendar, 'Immanuel Apollo...,' I booked this gig six weeks ago!"

Ben gets annoyed and indignant, and with 'in-your-face' sarcasm, reproves Immanuel.

Ben: "Ha! Dude..., I heard you..., and you're not scheduled! Now what is it about "NO" that you don't comprehend?"

Immanuel: "Look, I don't like your attitude and I'm not talking to a doorman! I want a word with the Owner!"

Ben: "Yeah, really? You just had one!"

Ben shuts the door with a smirk and leaves.

Immanuel punches the door in an outburst of anger. Hurting his hand, he blurts out in frustration and kicks some sidewalk garbage as he walks away.

Immanuel: "Lame ass bastards! Can't believe they pulled this shit on me again!"

Immanuel rants while passing by Ed who is sitting on the curb, watching what just happened with Immanuel. Ed had stumbled and fallen, and is having difficulty getting up on his own. He's scraped up and frumpled, watching intently as Immanuel passes.

Immanuel: "There... see? It's a fkn conspiracy against MEN, and if you're talented, it's open season for these bitches...!"

Immanuel walks on, then realizes that Ed fell and needs help. So he turns around to help dust him off and stand him up.

Ed: "Thanks. Much appreciated! It was a little demoralizing being crouched like a circus dwarf on this curb... Look, I saw what just went down, and I've gotta tell ya, you're damn right! I've been in this business for centuries, yet they still bust my hump when I try to book my artists in these clubs."

Immanuel: "I don't know who they are... or care about them. They're not me; maybe they suck!"

Ed: "Okay, I'll give you that; but it could also be you're not what their audience is hungry for!"

Immanuel: "Right, cause I'm not a member of the Castrati Choir!"

Ed: "Ah-hah..., here, take my card. I've been in music management for over forty years."

Ed rumples through his pockets then hands Immanuel a grubby business card.

Ed: "Ed Blazenberg, I used to be a household name... you heard of me...?"

Immanuel shakes his head sarcastically "NO".

Ed: "You're a little raw, but I like your style! Why don't you take that Uzi out and fire off a few rounds. Let me hear what ya got!"

Immanuel quickens and is alerted to the promotional opportunity; he plays Ed his soul song, **"Rainmaker's Rondo."**

Aimee and Roger meet to discuss business. A waiter comes over to hand out menus.

Roger: "I checked the press... the critics are already talking up your next series..."

Aimee: "But I don't have anything ready yet."

Roger: "Think organic and start painting; the inspiration will come. You've got to stay in motion."

Waiter: "Are you ready to order? Will you be having anything to drink?"

Roger: "In a moment..."

Roger then inquires about Immanuel.

Roger: "By the way..., that musician you were talking to at the gallery, what's his name? He looks familiar..., strikes a chord..."

Back on the street..., Immanuel finishes Ed's song amazing Ed, who then arranges to represent him as his new artist.

Ed: "You were right on! You're way too good for these dumps! In my entire career, I've never heard anyone do what you just did! You're... a kind of ... phenomenon..."

Immanuel smiles, murmurs, "Thanks", then puts his head down in secret shyness.

Ed: "Look, I've got some people I want you to meet... Call me. I can take you big time! But you gotta stick with me, 'cause in the wrong hands you'll end up in nowheresville!"

Aimee goes to her studio and lays out sheets of canvas; she looks at them to visualize Roger's idea for the new art series. She murmurs aloud...

Aimee: "If I could only paint love on canvas."

Immanuel goes to his dark, messy apartment, tears an eviction notice off his door and grumbles. Pictures of him all over the walls say he's the top rock star in the world, his empire built on bed romps with hungry dumped groupies and broken-hearted women.

He enters a private closet in the back of his apartment that is plastered with pictures over an altar of self-worship. He goes in to post a pic of Aimee as his new sacrifice. He sits back and reclines, drinks, smokes weed, lays out a line of cocaine, then watches computer porn. His cell rings, he answers while he's viewing; three women make separate bootie calls.

Immanuel talks to the actresses featured on the computer porn: "Filthy little whore... so you like it rough and nasty, don't you...?"

Then his phone rings and he speaks to the first woman calling for a sex date.

Woman in Heat: "Uhm..., it's been a while... miss me? What about tonight?"

Immanuel: "Sure, Sexy Lady..., a little busy, but you can slip in for a drink around midnight."

He returns to his drugs and computer porn as the phone rings again with the second woman calling for a bootie call.

Married Woman: "Are you coming? I haven't heard from you..."

Immanuel: "Yeah, I'll be by after breakfast... Just make sure he's left for work this time, I don't mind a close shave, but not a Sweeney Todd!"

He returns to the computer porn, acting out as if he's in the film, speaking to the actress.

Immanuel: "Naughty nympho, I'll spank your slutty ass!"

A third woman calls, interrupting his fantasy. She begs for a visit.

Woman in waiting: "What's keeping you so busy? Why do I have to wait so long to see you again? Damn! By the way..., did you find my pink lace bra under your bed? I left it for you...You want to know what you left for me? I had to take medicine again!"

Immanuel: "Hey Babe, just thinking about ya. Ah-ha, booty call tomorrow, midnight and moonlight. But seriously..., don't haul those overnight bags here again and embarrass yourself, Honey, this isn't a hot sheets hotel!"

He continues watching the porn movie and speaks vulgarities aloud, acting like he's at a rodeo.

Roger, while at home, is using his computer to investigate Immanuel. He speaks aloud:

Roger: "Small world, but you won't get away this time!"

Five

A clear, blue sky guides Immanuel to Aimee's studio where he waits in the doorway with a bouquet of flowers, intuitively knowing when she would leave for lunch.

Aimee: "Oh, Immanuel…, you surprised me!"

Immanuel: "I'm on my way to a private beach, a lush, verdant sanctuary where the sea effervesces as wedding champagne, and the golden sun sparkles like Cleopatra's diamonds as they tumble upon the frothy, undulating, crests of liberty that dance freestyle like gypsies, naked, unashamed."

Aimee looks at Immanuel, surprised though delighted. She smiles as he kisses her forehead.

Immanuel: "Join me; I'll be there in an hour."

He hands her the flowers and directions then keeps walking. She watches him slip away into the crowd.

In an hour she taxis to the cove. As she walks toward him, he greets her with outstretched arms, a warm smile, and gourmet picnic set on a table cloth.

They sit together and playfully feed each the delicacies laid out, flirting innocently back and forth.

Then they stand together to view the scenery. He steps up behind her, puts his hands on her hips and looks into her eyes with a deep, inquiring glance, soul-to-soul, as if to say: *"I really like you a lot. Do you think you might possibly be able to like me?"* She is taken back by this unexpected glance, surprised at the intensely passionate heart she sees hidden within him. She also sees his inner core of wisdom produced by an unknown source of suffering and torment from which he appeared to be begging for release.

Immanuel: "Ladylove, I realize that we're not family..., but it feels like we are..., or should be..."

Aimee: "Yeah..."

Something strange happened. When he touched her arm, they both felt it: as if they were made of one flesh, born of the same body like twins or siblings, or spouses who've been together for fifty years.

They go for a dreamy, romantic walk through winding country roads, gardens in full spring bloom, artful mansions set on coastal hillsides with glistening water views and emerald meadows of grazing horses. He stops to kiss her sweetly as the fragrance of Lilac pervades the air. They continue walking past rows of Honeysuckle, holding hands, and flirting playfully.

Immanuel lifts her up in his arms and carries her as a princess. He places her down beside a trellis festooned with red Roses where he hugs her before also laying down in some freshly cut grass. Behind an incensing Cedar grove is where they spoke their first warm passionate kiss. The lush fragrance of the living green fills them, as a Wisteria vine in the soft breeze reaches over and tickles them.

A powerful experience of divine confirmation, is when nature cooperates with love.

Aimee: "Oh..., Immanuel..., I feel all tingly..."

Immanuel: "Oooh..., woman, your pheromone perfume is mystifying! Uhm, are you exuding your primal essence deliberately for me?"

Later they sit down under the tree to feed each other the food and drink Immanuel laid out for them. She puts a strawberry in her mouth and passes it to him lip-to-lip. They tease and play with the wine and food as the sun sets a brilliant coral.

Immanuel: "A special time of day... when the Sun is exchanged for the Moon and darkness falls..."

Aimee: "Yeah..."

While sitting on the shore under the full moon, they cuddle romantically. His phone rings, he doesn't look, but tosses it aside in annoyance. He touches her with irresistible sensuality, she returns the affection. They kiss with blazing affection, penetrating beneath the armor people wear revealing a childlike emotional nakedness viewable only by one's unique soul mate.

Each time they recite a sacred verse to one another they fall into a different position emphasizing their words...

Immanuel: "Feels so good to hold you beneath this lonely, old lantern...it's the sign you were born under, isn't it?"

Aimee: "Yes..., how did you know?"

Immanuel: "Because I know you..., and that you could walk with me in black. It's your peaceful, silent spirit, mysterious..., unsearchable..., enchanting as the night."

Aimee: "Uhm..."

Immanuel: "Did you know we're inscribed among the stars? We're king and queen of the zodiac, an inferno of romance the world chases but never catches! Yet for us it's natural, effortless."

Two black cats wrestle into view, a male and female, they meow, growl, nuzzle, tussle then run by.

Aimee: "I don't know why, but I can't stop shaking."

Immanuel: "Do you believe in soul mates?"

Aimee: "Definitely…, but I have never met mine."

Immanuel: "What do you suppose he'd be like?"

Aimee: "Humn…, I imagine…"

Immanuel: "He'd have deep eyes? Like a lurid river that bathes you beneath its crimson moon?"

Aimee: "Yeah…, ascending to the sunny, gleaming gates of heaven opened up to forever…!"

They roll onto their sides, facing each other as their words are breathily exhaled.

Immanuel: "Yes…, for he'd see, adore, and complete you, the way no one else can or ever will?"

Aimee: "It's mysterious poetry of the heart: romantic love…, like a perfect cherry red valentine arriving late and full of bittersweet chocolates!"

He gently rolls over on top of her and looks in her eyes, probing her heart.

Immanuel: "Why bitter and not sweet? Why late and not now? "Kiss me with the kisses of your lips, for your love is sweeter than wine…"

Aimee: "That's from the Song of Solomon…"

Immanuel: "Do you know this one: "I am my beloved's and my beloved is mine"? … all mine… "O, my dove, in the secret place of the steep pathway, let me see your form, so lovely, and hear your sweet voice", … so sweet… It's okay, no one else is here…, take your clothes off…, uh…, soooo pretty…"

He rips off his shirt, belt, shoes, then goes for his pants but she stops him….

Aimee: "My beloved, whom my soul loves, is to me a pouch of myrrh which lies upon my heart between my nursing breasts all night long…"

Immanuel: "'Let me climb the palm tree of love and take hold of its fruit clusters'… Nice rack…, let me see it!"

He reaches for her breasts, slipping his hands up from her waist, but she stops him.

Aimee: "On my bed…, night after night in restless tears…, I long sought him whom my soul loves; but did not find him…"

She rolls onto her belly facing the water as he caresses her back and studies her form like he was sculpting a new Venus.

Immanuel: "'The curves of your hips are royal gems, the handiwork of a Master Artist. Your navel is a round goblet in which to swirl the finest wines... your luscious belly is a heap of harvest wheat fenced about with young lilies gazing on", dreaming of their own enraptured night beneath the starlight... Angel, take these off..."

He pulls her clothes, she resists. But then she turns over and wraps her arms and legs around him.

Aimee: "When I found my beloved, the one whom my soul loves, I held onto him and would not let him go..."

Immanuel: "I have come into my garden my sister in Spirit and my bride in life, let its spices be wafted abroad..., I have eaten my honeycomb and my honey..., and drunk all of its milk and its wine."

Aimee: "I adjure you, O handmaidens of the King, by the gazelles of the field, do not arouse or awaken my love, until the time so pleases..."

Immanuel: "Selah..., it's getting chilly... There must be a warm place we can hang?"

Aimee: "We could go back to my studio? I live there too; it's a super cool space."

He jumps up and packs all their stuff up while swatting mosquitos landing on him. They walk away, his phone rings, he ignores it.

Immanuel: "Great idea, let's roll. These bugs are ravenous, they'll devour us out here!"

Back at Roger's house he finally confirms it's Immanuel through his web research. He shouts aloud.

Roger: "Gotcha! How long I've labored for this fine day!"

He calls Mike, who is awakened from sleep beside a woman.

Roger: "Listen, Mike..., I know it's late, but can you pick up?"

Mike: "I'm unconscious..., can't this wait?"

Roger: "No! If he recognized me, he'll bolt."

Mike: "If 'who' recognized you...?"

Roger stands up and paces around the room...

Roger: "It's been eight dry years, but I finally found the prick, and unjustly, that bastard is alive and well."

Mike: "What bastard? There are so many..."

Mike rubs his eyes and turns on the nightlight.

Roger: "The scumbag who screwed my wife! And if you recall, his sadistic head games led to her suicide. Ah-ha..., that bastard!"

Mike: "Yeah, I get that you're dealing with a grave, unresolved tragedy..., but you can't assume their 'dingy affair' was the undisputed cause of her hari-kari..."

Roger stares out the window into the night.

Roger: "Are you serious? I recovered every text he sent LeAnn. It's clear that psycho feeds on the tortured suffering of his victims! It's time the scales of justice found rest. Are you in?"

Mike: "In...? Look tomorrow's a new day, when the sun rises on my coffee pot, I'll have a better chance of figuring out how to proceed... For tonight, nothing newsworthy, okay...? Get some sleep."

Mike rolls back over and turns off the light.

Roger: "I'm dead serious, Mike..., this isn't huddle bravado. That vampire sucked my lifeblood out; and I will get it back!"

Meanwhile Immanuel and Aimee get out of a taxi and walk to her studio apt.

Once inside..., Immanuel looks around in awe and envy. Her space is full of musical instruments, art, production equipment, cool furnishings, and interior architecture.

Immanuel: "Wow! Proper place to call home! Always wanted a loft like this..., bet it has great acoustics too."

Aimee: "Yeah, except for the tone deaf diva who 'figeros' opera in the stairs all night."

Immanuel sits down on the floor, leans against a post when his phone rings again. This time he looks to see who's calling, but ignores it. He gestures for her to walk over and sit down beside him. She does.

Immanuel: "Sweet..., gotta take this all in... What were you planning with these?"

He points to the canvases all around the floor.

Aimee: "Not sure, I was going to experiment with acrylic house paint, but until the idea arrives, all I can do is stare at it waiting for inspiration to spark!"

He relaxes with her a moment then kisses her and takes her hand to dance. He begins to hum a song then turns on her sound system. He leads her in dance through a progressive series of styles...

Immanuel: "Uhm.., Now this is what inspires me! I love dance; it's like we're painting with our feet. I feel so alive when music pulses through my body, I don't care what style..., it's all good if you translate it right..."

They move through a variety of Latin dances: Salsa, Tango, Rumba... until he starts knocking over the open paint cans she left on the floor.

Aimee: "Uh-oh, be careful, I think you just kicked over the Magenta; uh, there goes the Scarlet.."

While kicking over the cans, they step in the acrylics, body painting the canvases she laid on floor.

Immanuel: "You're one blazing hot goddess! Do you have any idea what you're doing to me?"

He lifts her and dances across the room with her in his arms. They kiss as he lays her down on a blank canvas. They continue kissing and rolling all over the floor, removing articles of clothing as they roll, until they are nude, dancing through a series of horizontal positions and stopping every few turns, imprinting the canvases with the sensual stages and sexual body language of love. She resists having sex entirely, intercourse, which amuses him as they roll around in the paint. This becomes her new art series.

Sir

Disheveled but contented, Immanuel walks to his late morning appointment, his guitar strapped on his back with a cigarette in his mouth. He smiles at women passing by who flirt back. While checking the time on his phone, it rings again; he looks to see who is calling, then ignores it.

When he reaches the corner of Houston Street and Sixth Avenue, he stops. A yellow taxi pulls up in front of him, as Ed struggles to open the door.

Ed: "Immanuel, sorry I'm a bit late; jump in!"

Immanuel sees Ed then flips his cigarette away and jumps in.

Ed: "Can you believe it took me over twenty minutes to hail a cab? You'd think the damn Pope was in Town!"

Immanuel: "Tsk-tsk, that obscenity will cost you three 'Hail Marys'!"

Ed: "Ha-ha! How 'bout a 'Hail Mary' pass? Ha! At least you got a sense of humor! It's required reading in this business."

Immanuel looks out the window pondering...

Immanuel: "Thanks. So you really think I'm what they're looking for?"

Ed: "Money's what they're looking for! My job is to make them see you as a rough-cut diamond waiting to be set in platinum...; you gotta show up like a better investment than all the other idol wanna-bes out there, surfing the golden jetstream from coast to coast... Music's a rough game, Kid. You're not the only unemployed, over-cooked, teenage rock star beating the drum for a tour bus with his name on it. You're gonna have to come across strong, like you're fighting for your life!"

Immanuel: "Screw the coin machine; I'm an artist! I hate the commercial industry and how it makes writers whore themselves out. Haven't you noticed how much better the music is before an artist is signed to a label?"

Ed: "Cut the Crap! You know damn well it doesn't matter if you've got it; if you can't sell it..., it's worthless! It's about the bottom line: no market plus no audience equals no sales! Be realistic: it used to be a dime a dozen for guys like you; now it's six dozen for a nickel!"

Immanuel continues looking out the window and sees musicians all over the City who are playing, begging, hanging out, and walking by as the taxi ride continues to their business appointment.

While they talk Ed slaps and rubs Immanuel's thigh. He looks at Ed surprised with trepidation and moves away to slip his hand off.

Ed: "So tell me..., you do believe in yourself, don't you...? Or am I blowing the paltry remainder of my time account on a loser?"

As Immanuel moves over, squeezing himself against the door, glaring out the window, Ed tries again.

Ed: "Don't worry, the man on top isn't gay."

Uptown in Central Park Aimee talks about her new love to Clara. While walking in the Park they pass a group of protestors demonstrating against the horse-drawn carriages. Agreeing with the cause they join in for an hour, then continue their stroll.

Clara: "You really don't care that I'm part Cherokee, do you...?"

Aimee: "Of course I care..., it's just that I've been distracted by an amazing man. Gosh..., I wish they'd treat these horses kindly, like family..."

Clara: "Amazing...? What's so great about him?"

Aimee: "Everything! I think I'm in crazy love... I've never felt like this before."

Clara: "Uh-oh... When it seems too good to be true... guess what? "

Aimee: "Don't be a pessimist! You haven't even seen him yet... look... he's really cute..."

Aimee goes through her phone to find some photos... Clara looks intently at his pictures, but sees something about Immanuel that makes her uneasy.

Clara: "I don't think so; I'm getting a major 'player' vibe from him.... Don't fall for his game! He probably uses music to seduce women."

Aimee: "Clara..., Immanuel proposed to me!"

Clara: "Oh, please…, marriage? How long have you been seeing him..., a month?"

Aimee: "When it's right, you can feel it. He's my soul mate! I gave him the keys to my studio!"

Clara: "Don't you think you should get to know him before you start giving your life away? I'm surprised at you! You're always so cautious..."

Immanuel and Ed arrive at the production meeting. They walk in together. Steve Landau is on his conference phone arguing with another client's manager. He gestures for them to take a seat near his desk. Then, he swivels away and turns his back to them to finish his discussion.

Landau is a music promoter and head of a record label that has several Platinum albums and CDs on the market. But he's older and hasn't had a hit in more than ten years. He's struggling to stay in the rapidly changing market, but has become another hardened arts and entertainment executive trying to navigate around the new face of the industry.

Steve: "That's not the point, Don, he's your artist. I would never sign him! He needs shock therapy; he's not living in real time... His last gig drew 200 people, and he sold under 10,000 music junkies on i-Tunes. You know I can't work with numbers like that..!"

Immanuel looks over at Ed nervously. Ed winks at Immanuel as if to say, "I told you so." Steve hangs up the phone and turns his attention to them.

Steve: "Next case... I've only got about two minutes..., so let's hear it..., hit me with your best subway panhandle..."

Ed: "Right-O...! Manny's a treasure I found in the gutter, and his music speaks for itself. Come on, Apollo, show 'em what you got!"

47

Immanuel takes up his guitar and plays Steve's soul song called: **"Copperhead Musketeer"**.

Steve: "Nice..., sounds familiar though..."

Ed: "Because it's your soul song, Steve!"

Steve: "No, I mean, the chord pattern is too common, sounds like several other tunes. There's nothing original anymore, everybody's copying and stealing. But I'm assuming you're not some one-hit wonder and you've got more material. So why don't you play me your own song, so I can hear if you're a winner or a bummer!"

Ed: "Manny was adopted. He doesn't know his parents, let alone his song. I'm sure people will buy his release without it..."

Steve: "Maybe they will, but I won't! I need your song! That would be your only hope to grab a marketing hook! The 'cult of personality' thang, ya know..."

Ed sits on the edge of his seat; Steve gets up, sits on the edge of his desk, and looks down at them.

Ed: "But what about his original style?"

Steve: "It's passable, MAYBE, if packaged right. But it's still risky... he's an unknown and he's aged out of the pop rock demographic."

Ed squirms in his seat, Steve folds his arms across his chest and purses his lips in skeptic review.

Ed: "What about concerts, if he starts filling up some halls and builds a following?"

Steve saunters back to his leather chair, plops down, and puts his feet on the desk, soles facing them.

Steve: "Thought he already had one..., NO? Why are you bringing me people like this?"

Ed: "We just need a little time..."

Steve leans forward aggressively challenging them to prove Immanuel is worth money.

Steve: "Time? You know how much time, labor, and money it's going to cost me to launch someone like him into commercial orbit? Without ample investment, guaranteed he'll be DOA!"

Ed: "No way..., Apollo's the real deal; he'll sell, he's got talent!"

Steve: "Really? If so, he should be able to pack the house at the top ten venues, develop a loyal nationwide fan base, and bring me his song in six weeks, then we can revisit the options. As it stands, I wouldn't stick a penny in his navel!"

Steve spits on a penny, holds it up laughing, then sticks it on his arm. He stands up to shake hands but his phone rings, so he sits back down, swivels his back to them, and takes the call instead. Immanuel's phone rings, he looks at it and ignores it. They both stand up and leave feeling dejected.

They remain silent as they leave the building. Then while standing outside the building Ed tries to console a discouraged Immanuel.

Ed: "My connections may help with the clubs but you gotta write your song, Manny!"

Immanuel: Don't call me Manny! My name's Immanuel! And forget that song! How can I sing about my purpose when I don't know who I am?"

Ed: "Then you've only got one choice: you'll have to find your birth parents; they've got to be out there somewhere..."

Ed waves for a taxi and one pulls up right away. He holds the door open for Immanuel, but he declines the ride, pissed off. Ed lights up a cigar and drives off in the cab. Immanuel lights up a joint and smokes weed while walking away murmuring aloud.

Immanuel: "Time wasting fkn losers, whores, with their heads up their butts, don't know shit about what music is!"

Seven

Immanuel and Aimee are doing couples yoga: stretching, bending, twisting, and intertwining before breakfast.

Immanuel: "Why the cold shoulders, Princess? How come you won't have sex with me?"

Aimee: "I want to, but I'm not officially yours yet..."

Immanuel: "Oh, come now... I know you've got a bad girl hiding in there..., when you gonna let her join the party?"

Aimee: "Sorry. I'm keeping the baby's room clean!"

Immanuel: "Just as well... Most guys want a good girl for the long haul."

Aimee gives him a skeptical look and sighs, as if to say: 'even guys like you?'

Immanuel: "Seriously! We all want beautiful, elegant trophy wives who will be faithful, grace our homes, and raise geniuses for us."

Aimee: "Sounds more like a job description than a mutually-affirming, personal relationship."

Immanuel: "Maybe, but we can only truly love the good girl."

Aimee: "Why? I'd have thought the opposite."

Immanuel: "We may fall for the bad girl with crazy, obsessive desire and be willing to do anything, even kill, to gain her love and acceptance..., but deep down we know what she is."

Aimee: "You'd allow someone to provoke you to violence?"

Immanuel: "These women really know how to manipulate us, let me tell you..."

Aimee: "If you know the game, why do you let them play you like a puppet?"

She stretches her legs apart and reaches out to hold his hands, placing his feet against her calves. She leans back and stretches him forward to work his hamstrings and lower back, while staying on topic.

Immanuel: "A few reasons: 1st, we're stupid!"

Aimee: "Sounds like a cop out..."

Immanuel: "No really, trust me, we are!"

Aimee: "Conveniently dumb, perhaps. Even still it can't only be that..."

Immanuel: It isn't. It's also because she's the unattainable standard, and if we can turn an ice queen into a hot lover, we raise our rank among other men."

Aimee: "Do you possibly realize how teenage that sounds?"

Immanuel: "Of course..., but it never changes. We'll think like that until they close the cover."

Aimee leans forward to push him backward while she stretches her legs and back.

Aimee: "Are those the primary motivations?"

Immanuel: No..., we also want the forbidden fruits and the ones we can't have... tastes better when you nail 'em!"

Aimee: "Aahh-haa..., I'll keep that in mind."

Immanuel: "There is one other reason..."

They do the last stretching position, seated on the floor back-to-back. She leans backward against him pushing him forward to put his head to his knees.

Aimee: "I'm not sure I want to know."

Immanuel: "Actually you may appreciate this one: we aspire to be heroes. The good girl is okay and doesn't need to be saved from her own foibles."

Aimee: "To me, this is the worst injustice of all!"

Immanuel: "How so?"

Aimee: "It's the good girls who hurt the most and deserve to be rescued from the heartless betrayals and rejections that we are continually impacted by."

Immanuel: "You're not the only soul that feels the pain of this existence..."

Aimee: "It's different... we're the ones with the real feelings!"

Immanuel: "How distastefully presumptuous of you, my Dove!"

Aimee: "Oh, please, you know it's true! But it doesn't matter because you find bad girls more exciting anyway. You'll probably marry one..."

Immanuel: "Marry a girl like that? It'll never happen! How can I adore someone who doesn't value herself? No genuine respect, no real love!"

Aimee: "If you feel that way, why would you chase after them?"

Immanuel: "'Because they're a huge turn on: easy, exciting, lusty, unpredictable, and empowering like a testosterone shot, and don't mind getting dirty."

She stretches him past his comfort zone...

Immanuel: "Ouch!"

Aimee: "STDs and all...?"

She twists him into an uncomfortable position.

Immanuel: "Ease up! Okay... that's enough for this muscle group!"

Aimee: "Guess you don't know that emotional pain hurts worse than physical pain..."

Immanuel: "Pain is not something I give any mental space to no matter whose it is... see, I'm fair."

Aimee: "Fair is one grade above poor!"

Immanuel: "Yes, teacher. But I'm telling the truth here: I'd never marry a slut. Even though she's like a rite of passage, teaching us how to prevail over the dark side of life; she's really a human toilet bowl into which men relieve themselves of every angry, self-hating, insecure quirk they're ashamed to reveal in the presence of anyone else. She's the battlefield we fight other men on to establish our social rank."

Aimee: "That's horribly misogynistic! Scary to hear you think of any woman that way, regardless of her moral proclivities ..."

Their yoga becomes strained and contorted, more like a wrestling match between contestants than the sensual bodywork of lovers...

Immanuel: "No, dear..., it's obvious you don't get it... Men are wild and they instinctively reject and feel at enmity with civilization because it's always trying to castrate us and turn us into nice femmy-boys who behave themselves."

Aimee wraps her thighs around his waist and stretches him backward while trying to unravel his perspective.

Immanuel: "Whereas the bad girl, being more like a man in a woman's body, encourages us to let our inner bad boy run amuck in the untamed fields of sexual adventure long past the dinner bell. She knows the game and plays along."

Aimee: "And you simply cannot live without this?"

Immanuel: "Eventually we relinquish it! We don't stay with her. The life she offers isn't the one we really want, and as you said, it's not the real deal! In our hearts, we don't feel at home in her jungle."

Aimee: "Why?"

Immanuel: "Because it's sexual theater. In the light of day she's repulsive and comes up way short on comfort, status, achievement, and the warmth of the place we all seek – home!"

Aimee: "I appreciate your dissertation, but it sounds like a sport with lots of collateral damage."

Immanuel: "Hey, love is like war, when one falls, the other charges on to victory!"

She squeezes her legs. He coughs.

Immanuel: "There's another thing women don't get about us: men live in the black and white world of confounding mechanisms and fearsome amphitheaters where the threat of public humiliation, even total annihilation, perpetually looms."

Aimee: "I agree, seems like men react more out of inner fears and anxiety, whereas women react more to a sense of fairness, justice, and equality...."

Immanuel: "Yeah, but men are into revenge, it's harder for us to forgive and forget. Yet what I'm talking about here is different, it actually runs much deeper than that: males are unable to see colors, smell aromas, taste, feel, or hear as acutely as females do."

Aimee: "Yes, I read some of that research..."

Immanuel: "Cool, so then you'll get it when I say women provide access to the Garden of Eden for us. When we enter in, and not just physically, our senses and hearts come alive more than at any other time in our lives. This makes women and their innate capacities terrifying to us. They have the power to literally guard the gates between life and death."

Aimee sits up and hugs him for comfort. Then he walks over, picks up his guitar and begins to strum a song about what they just discussed... Unable to find the right lead in lyric line, he picks a few lead lines and continues talking.

Immanuel: "You know men always remember that one gorgeous girl from High School?"

Aimee: "Yes, I've heard their laments..."

Immanuel: "Okay..., but do you know why...? She's our gateway girl! As soon as we stop hating females and rejecting Mommy, she appears."

Aimee: "Yeah ... and...?"

Immanuel: "It happens when we first emerge into manhood, she mystically shows up, bigger than life, and every bit as promising..."

Aimee wonders whose 'gateway girl' she may have been... if any...

Immanuel: That fascination is the strongest occasion we'll ever experience with a woman... until one of them actually gives birth to our son. So we never forget her, and always wonder what life would have been like, 'if'... we'd hooked up with her."

Aimee stares at the ceiling in melancholia.

Immanuel: "Here's another thing: what you see now appears like just another rogue male. But we all start out as innocent, simple, little boys who just want to play around and find adventures to tell the world about. It's when puberty strikes that the whole playing field changes. That's when we learn what it really means to shift gears from being a boy to a man. Women have no clue what this is about..."

Aimee: "I agree! Even if I live to be 100, I'll still never be able to fully understand the male mind."

Immanuel: "Women emerge into our society through the bond they have with their mothers. They don't have to reject their primary caregiver because they will grow up to be like her. Not so for boys. And if the boy's father is absent, competitive, or rejecting, he will have no scaffolding to erect his manhood on."

Aimee: "Women, as mothers..., get this..."

Immanuel: "No they don't!"

Aimee: "Solo moms do effectively raise sons!"

Immanuel: "It doesn't matter... The strongest love bond on Earth is the one shared between a father and his son..., that's when it's good!"

Aimee: "What about his soul mate?"

Immanuel: "See what I'm saying? You don't get us at all! Whatever a man does in life is ultimately to please his dad so he'll make him proud enough to pass the baton of inheritance and grant succession rights. But if his father is uncaring, absent, neglectful, critical, ridiculing, competitive, shameful, or if he shuts his son out, it will damage his core. He could react in any number of ways, from anger to denial."

Aimee: "What about all the contributions that mothers make? You talk as if they don't matter at all!"

She gets up and starts moving a shelving unit from one wall to another...

Immanuel: "They have an influence but a man gains his sense of self from his father. I'm not going to candy coat this! If he feels secure in the world, it is mostly from what his father imparted to him. Why? Because the world of men is a fearsome place! Think about it: we compete, mock, replace, beat, kill, rape, rob, shame, blame, game, and in an infinite number of ways, outdo and emasculate each other! If a man is not equipped from youth to meet the arduous task of social emergence, he could face a brutal outcome."

Aimee: "Why do men force these rules on each other?"

Immanuel: "We don't really want it, but we have to. That's what it means to be a man. Carnivores don't really want to have to kill. If fed and cared for, they will peaceably cohabitate with their vegetarian prey. They'd rather dwell without carnage, but their biology and circumstances drives them to it."

Aimee: "I've always believed that. The food chain is such a sad aspect of the world!"

Immanuel walks over, sits next to Aimee and looks into her inquiring eyes as he shares his secret attraction by petting her head and kissing her.

Immanuel: "Don't hate it, Aimee, just make it better.... for all of our sakes!"

She puts her head on his shoulder.

Immanuel: "You want to know another reason why men are afraid of women...? Because we're still sweet, scared, little boys inside... And a lot of women are kind of cold and evil inwardly, witchy, dark..., I'd even say..., ugly! When we discover this accidentally after pursuing a beautiful package on the outside, it messes us up. This is secretly traumatizing to men, and it's why we can never really bond to the majority of women we meet."

Aimee: "Is that reality... or something men perceive about women because of their own fears?"

Immanuel: "No! No way! Trust me..., you can't believe what some women have asked me for!"

Aimee: "Okay, but no one said you had to go for it!"

Immanuel: "Men are innately stupid when it comes to self-protection. Ever see guys on a toxic work site? You're not gonna see them wearing all the protective gear. We always think that because we're men, nothing can hurt us, even though we're so afraid of everything inwardly, we deal with it by acting like it doesn't exist. And that's how we get nailed by it. We always think we have a higher threshold than we actually do. To prove to ourselves, and whoever else, that we are real men, we'll take on any challenge put before us, even though repeated exposure eventually gets us so angry that we act out in some weird way."

Aimee starts cleaning the floor..., he paces.

Aimee: "Why does it get you angry?"

Immanuel: "Come on..., that's obvious..., you can answer that one yourself!"

Aimee: "No, really..., I don't get it..."

Immanuel: "I told you..., we're still little boys and we adored our innocence. We're extremely angry at everything that has stolen it from us and we take it out on each other and on whoever happens to get in the way! We need a male mentor who will empower us to reach the top, and an adoring female love: pure like an angel, nurturing as a mother, and awesome like a goddess. Instead we consistently find Pharaohs and demon witches. Wouldn't that piss you off?"

Aimee walks to the kitchen to make breakfast.

Aimee: "Yeah, I hear the anger. Honestly, I do find the duality of men tough to navigate through."

Immanuel: "All men are two people under the same skin. Often one doesn't know about or like the other. We're not integrated the way women are. It's a chromosomal thing because we have to fight, defend, and do horrible things yet still be able to nurture and be compassionate. That's why there's this wall in our brains... Women are XX and your brains can multi-task. But men are XY. The X is cool about building the house, but the Y wants to tear it down! And these two guys don't know how to talk to each other. For some, can really be a problem!"

Aimee: "What's your solution?"

Immanuel: "You, Polymath, you're my muse!"

Aimee: "How can you be sure?"

Immanuel: "I've never been more sure!"

Aimee: "Well..., you certainly did sound very professorial in this conversation..."

Immanuel: "That's what I'm saying..., I've always wanted someone I could talk to like this... But I've had trouble finding it. By the way, how much you think we'll get for our sex-on-canvas art series?"

Aimee: "Depends what the market will bare!"

Immanuel: "Ha! Good one...! We're splitting that, right? The money? My butt is plastered all over those canvases just as much as your plump derriere is, right Honeypot? "

Roger texts her about the exhibition. After checking it, she informs Immanuel.

Aimee: "Roger just texted me; I have to help him set up. Be cool if you could stop by tonight..."

Immanuel: "Oh, I forgot..., I've got a gig. By the way, is Roger's last name, Falcone?"

While she's getting ready to leave, she walks away and doesn't hear his question. He gets a call from another woman, he answers it, then checks his pocket coke vile. He books a bootie call.

Eight

Later that afternoon, Immanuel is walking uptown looking for something to do when Ed calls.

Immanuel: "Landau change his mind?"

Ed: "Not yet, but I've got a few solid bookings for you today. Look.., I know it's short notice, but we can't afford to drag our asses."

Immanuel: "Okay, I'll go. Text me the info."

Meanwhile as Aimee and Roger set up the art for display, Roger gets a text invite and reads it aloud.

Roger: "Southampton Filmmakers, VIP party huh... I'll arrange for you to perform, they're always interested in new soundtracks."

Immanuel arrives at a spot where he's booked to play. It's a group of senior citizens celebrating one of their eightieth birthdays. He is greeted at the door by an aged host who escorts him in.

Elder Host: "Well..., bet you thought we'd be the "rat pack" heh-heh! Okay, wake up, everybody... Music's here! You must be the nice young Sinatra Eddie sent over to entertain us... "

Immanuel: "I hope not! But if I am..., I'm not really here... please forget my name like everything else..."

Back at the Gallery guests are arriving. Roger greets them as they are directed to the refreshments.

Immanuel finished his first booking quickly and goes to his second gig which is in a small off-off-Broadway theater. He speaks aloud to himself, then bangs on the door. The Manager answers.

Immanuel: "This isn't sooo bad, wonder what the headcount is? It's gotta be at least 200..." "Hey Man, should I enter and exit through the stage door out back?"

Manager: "I'm sorry, whatever your name is, doesn't your agent call you? We didn't sell any tickets for your show. It's lights out for the evening."

The Manager closes the door with an annoyed expression. Immanuel kicks the door and walks away, angrily speaking aloud.

Immanuel: "What the fck! Even a total dump like this?"

He walks away with his hands shaking from anger. He fumbles to light up a joint as his phone rings. A woman, Sharon, calls to make a bootie call appointment for now.

Sharon: "Your naughty, little girl is feeling very bored, love..."

Immanuel: "Okay, Sharon, but I don't have much time; I'm rocking a packed house later..."

He walks to the subway and goes uptown to her apartment.

That evening at the show, Aimee is standing around speaking with Critics while Roger promotes her work. She keeps looking around for Immanuel.

Clara is walking around the City with some artist friends when she sees Immanuel kissing Sharon who he just had sex with. They're standing in front of the bar he was shut out of previously. There's an Open Mic Night sign in the window. Clara recognizes him from the photos Aimee showed her, so she hangs out to watch what he's up to.

Immanuel: "Kitchen table was sooo hot... Remember me.., when you eat off of it again..."

He smacks her butt, sends her away then goes into the bar to play a few songs.

He signs up to play by crossing off someone else's name while a guitarist is on stage. Noisy place, busy night, so he put himself ahead in the line up.

While scanning the room, he sees a woman, Donna, drunk on other side of bar, and targets her for the night's score.

The open Mic host, Ben, didn't notice when Immanuel stole someone's spot, so he announces the next performer, and then finds himself preventing a fight from erupting.

Ben: "Nice set, let's give it up for Jesmond Tanner... Next performer..., Immanuel Apollo...?"

Darver Klemenstadt, who was signed in ahead of Immanuel, sees it, gets angry, goes up aggressively and starts to play, when Immanuel pulls his plug out and plugs it into his own guitar. Clara watches the scenario unfold. Ben steps away but watches before being sure what's going on and how to intervene.

Darver: "No way, Man, wait up, I'm next! He scratched my name off. Dude, this your first time here? 'Cause that's a NO do!"

Immanuel: "I don't have time for people who can't handle their alcohol... I'm rocking now, toy-boy, and I've got a real performance in about an hour..., know what I'm saying?"

Darver: "Get your arrogant ass the fk off this stage! This is my audience! They show up for me!"

Ben: "Apollo just play and go... and make this your last time here... Carol, can Darver take your spot?"

Carol: "Yeah..., sure..., Ben. I'm cool with that. I don't have any new songs to do tonight anyway; so whatever you gotta do..."

Immanuel plugs in and sings a seduction song for the lonely, drunk woman squirming at the bar. She primps herself to look hot. After the song, he straps on his guitar and goes over to pick up Eleanor.

Immanuel: (to bartender) "Give her another of whatever she's been drinking..." (to her) "I can't imagine how a woman that looks like you..., WOW, uhm, is here..., alone, on a Saturday night just waiting around to meet a rock star like me..."

Eleanor: "My boyfriend threw me out..."

Immanuel: "Huh..., there's no accounting for taste, or the lack of it..., is there, Princess...?"

A Spanish woman, Hortense, sitting on the other side of the bar comes over to Immanuel. He ushers her away, so as to not disturb his seduction of Eleanor. She speaks to him with a strong accent.

Hortense: "I like your music. If you want to record a CD, I can help you out."

Immanuel: "Thanks! Some other time maybe."

He turns back to Eleanor who gets annoyed at Hortense's intrusion and gets up to leave with him.

Immanuel leaves with Eleanor, Clara leaves her friends and follows him. Hortense also follows him. He returns to the studio for a fling with Eleanor. Clara watches their interaction and shoots video and pictures, then hides until they emerge.

At the Gallery, Roger and Aimee are closing down after a very successful night. He turns the lights out and leaves, but she stays a little longer waiting around outside for Immanuel to show up...

Roger: "I prefer you didn't stand alone on the street, who knows how long. Can I drop you home?"

Aimee: "He's probably around the corner. But thanks. You did a fabulous job tonight. I don't know what I'd do if you ever retired..."

Roger: "Fear not, I'll never leave you. We've got too much we haven't done yet. Listen..., call me if you need me."

Roger leaves and Aimee checks the time on her phone, looking around for Immanuel to arrive. A murky homeless man passes in an intimidating way; she steps aside hoping he'll leave. He takes a few more steps, but then decides to park himself right in front of the gallery where she is standing periodically saying things to harass her.

Murky Man: "Ah-huh, Lady, I seen you before. You live here? You must got some money."

Meanwhile Immanuel leaves the studio with Eleanor, whose clothes are half off, hair a mess, skirt twisted, blouse open, and she's still drunk but happy.

Eleanor: "That was fun. When can we do it again?"

Immanuel: "You crazy witch! Just GO before the sun comes up and I see what you really look like! Eech! No wonder your boyfriend dumped you! Get the hell away from me before I catch a nasty disease, you disgusting, stupid tramp! A lousy lay too! You suck in bed. And you smell bad! Don't you wash?"

Eleanor is stunned, confused, and starts crying... He shoves her into a taxi so she won't remember where she was.

He runs to pick up Aimee who is now being intimidated by the murky man.

Murky Man: "Oohh, you look nice too. You wanna get together?"

Just then she sees Immanuel round the corner, so she runs to him and jumps into his arms.

Immanuel: "Love of my life, behold, I have come!

Aimee: "Oh…, Immanuel…, I miss you…"

Immanuel: "Miss you too! Sorry I'm late, gig ran overtime. But they dug me, couldn't get enough."

They share an electrified kiss: long, slow, and deep, then walk home holding hands. His phone rings and though he looks at it, he ignores it.

Immanuel: "Sold everything?"

Aimee: "Yes, the series was huge! People were bidding over the paintings."

Immanuel: "Nice! At full bounty?"

Aimee: "Actually…, over asking price!"

Immanuel: "Sweet!"

Aimee: "Yeah.., we're such an amazing team… Everybody says so.., and I can feel it too, a little more every time…"

They arrive home at the loft, continue their discussion…

Immanuel: "You know, love, I was wondering about something you alluded to… Do you really think being an artist is in our genes?"

Aimee: "Definitely, think about it. The soul is a product of our genes; it's created at the moment of conception, though no one knows exactly how yet..., Whereas, art is the poetic, inspirational language of the soul, especially true for the dialects of music... So it has to be!"

Immanuel: "What about if a man was going to succeed or fail? Couldn't that result from the karma his parents wrote into his lineage? A child might win or lose just because of what they did or didn't do, then spend his entire life spinning his wheels and never know why, nor be able to set things straight..."

Aimee: "In a way... It's because everything is inscribed into our DNA: all of our personal actions, environmental influences, and ancestral inheritances. But even with that, we can still choose to change generational curses into blessings."

Immanuel: "How? How can damn curses ever be broken, removed, or changed? It sucks if we can't escape the shit in our heritage! There must be a way around it..."

Aimee: "For better or worse, it's all part of your personal symphony, like a musical score..."

Immanuel: "Poetic, but senseless! I can't sign on to that! I'm going out for a smoke..."

Nine

When Immanuel walks outside the building, Hortense is waiting in the shadows for him. She steps out and blocks his passage; he tries to go around her.

Immanuel: "Excuse me!"

Hortense: "I told you, I can make it happen, but you have to believe me! The spirits put the right people in your way just when you need them."

Immanuel: "I don't need anybody! And yeah..., you're in my way..."

Hortense: "Your way is my way! Hortense Caballero."

She reaches to shake his hand, as a black limo pulls up. A sexy, raven-haired dominatrix, Mistrix Mayhem, opens the back door and stands up to invite him in. Hortense takes his arm and walks him toward it. They get in, drive away.

Hortense: "Mistrix Mayhem will be your escort. If you really want to make it in music, you have to know the right people and play by their rules..."

The car continues to the lower west side and turns down an alleyway. They all get out. Immanuel is escorted downstairs to a sex dungeon. There are small, peculiar stages with odd fixtures lining a long hallway leading to a dark room. People are engaged in strange sexual activity, dressed in various kinds of fetish attire. Disquieting sounds are heard through the smoky red light, with bodies strewn about, leading to the temple altar where high Priestess Plentavo awaits him. She is dressed in a metallic, Space Age, Marie Antoinette, Bride of Frankenstein, gothic costume with foot-high platform boots in a blue lighted room.

Priestess Plentavo: "You know me! Time we've met! She's making you weak! Thinning your blood! It's undrinkable! Makes me gag!"

She coughs up, spits at him. He jumps back.

Priestess Plentavo: "There's but one marriage even I cannot divide asunder: SEX and MUSIC! You do neither well! And you have failed to stir the caldron of the great orgy... the grand, worldwide hellbender!"

Plentavo steps out from behind the altar and stomps over to a large burning pot. She stirs it while looking at him aggressively. Plentavo moves in weird, angular ways, imposing threatening innuendos toward him. As she castigates him, others hear and mock. Hortense and Mayhem stand on either side of him as he listens to her pointed accusations and dictates.

Plentavo lambasts Immanuel with capricious sarcasm and venomous contempt shifting her mood and intonation with rapid, unpredictable gestures.

Priestess Plentavo: "If you keep hoarding rebellion to yourself..., you'll get NOTHING! Time to SMASH your worthless valentine and SPIN THE VORTEX! This is your assignment for the world! Hungry...? Then turn my boots to bread! Oh, so... sapless? Meathouse, give him someone to eat!"

Plentavo lifts a huge leg of raw meat overhead like a club, slams it on the altar, and ignites a fire as a big, imposing muscular dungeon master comes with others to usher a nervous Immanuel into the orgy room with revelers awaiting. They chant rhetorically: "**Spin the vortex**, spin the vortex" repeatedly as he is led away.

Ten

Aimee is at the Lab talking to Clara on the phone about her relationship with Immanuel. Robert acts nonchalant as he sneaks around to listen in.

Clara: "Hey Girl..., where's your feral mancat? Did he ever make it home last night?"

Aimee: "Yeah..., he came back this morning. Weird..., I had this crazy dream where I saw him in some sinister place..."

Dalisay bursts into Aimee's office, takes the Ipod from her ears and blurts out some confidential information that Robert eavesdrops on...

Dalisay: "Guess what? I found a mathematical geneticist who can regress DNA lines for centuries."

Aimee: "Gotta go, Clara, I'll call you later... Great, Dalisay, is his work published?

Dalisay: "Yes, it is..... mind if I pull it up on your screen? I checked it out before, quite amazing, really..., and in line with what we're looking into..."

She hangs up and they look over the studies on her computer.

Aimee: "Sure, let's take a look."

Dalisay: "I was able to speak with Dr. Simon about our research he emailed this to us. Hope you don't mind, I needed a sample, so I used his theory to analyze the DNA collected from you and Immanuel. Guess what it revealed?"

Aimee: "Yeah...? What?"

Dalisay: "You have a common ancestral root dating back to King Solomon, over 700 BC, and you also have an ideal complementation of chromosomal harmony. This is the unusual kind of pattern you'd only find in siblings, essentially twins, or soul mates."

Aimee: "Seriously? Hah..., then it is true!"

Dalisay: "And there's something else... that vibration..., the one we observed during fertilization is actually an organized pattern of tones. And each series appears unique to the individual. I replicated the experiment several times with both, humans and animals, but found no distinction between them. All species have it..., whatever it is..."

Aimee: "It's a song, isn't it?"

Dalisay: "I suppose..., could be..."

Dalisay notices Robert eavesdropping, so she goes inside and closes the office door. However they don't know that Robert hooked up a listening device which he activated to listen in.

Dalisay: "Also something amazing happened while I was watching the frequency..., it transformed into a silent body of light, filled up the embryo, then took its shape."

Aimee: "Wow! Do you know what you saw? You're probably the first person to ever observe this."

Dalisay: "I'd have to say it was some type of living sonoluminescence when sound becomes light and in this case..., the inanimate became animated! Also it was that ghostly bluish white color."

Aimee: "Oh my God! That's it: the creation of an individual soul!"

Dalisay: "Incredible! Have we really seen this? It's one of the most elusive things on Earth..."

Robert is actively listening in from his office.

Aimee: "Yes, that was it! We must replicate this experiment and videotape the process. Apparently every soul, whether human or animal, begins as a song, then it turns into the soul, a non-corporeal body of light that dwells, like a flame, within the physical body... a progression akin to sonoluminescence..."

Dalisay: "Wonder what the songs sound like?"

Meanwhile, in a downtown studio Immanuel and Ed are working with a record producer, Gilberto, that Ed had connections with. They are trying to record some of Immanuel's originals, but everything keeps going wrong. After six hours of trying to get it right, a dispute erupts.

Immanuel: "Dude, I don't sing with that much reverb. And the mid-range is off. I'm a baritone, not a falsetto."

Gilberto: "All your vocal tracks are flat and pitchy, your guitar rhythms are not in sync with the click, and your leads lines are off key. So the reason we're not getting anywhere is because you don't sound like you know where you're trying to take this song..."

Immanuel: "I wrote this hit fkn song! You're gonna tell me I don't know what it is?"

Gilberto: "How many times do I need to say it: we need to bring in some session musicians to lay down fill tracks... bass, percussion, keys... and some of these songs need edgy dance beats! You can't just drone out these old ballads, they're not what music is doing today. It's all about mixing genres, cultures, styles, and world rhythms especially! Fusion, Man!"

Immanuel: "You're not a musician, don't tell me what to say and how to speak it to the world!"

Ed: "Gil's right, Immanuel, just let him work before I have a coronary..."

Immanuel: "Dude, you're not hearing me! That's not what I do! I don't care about appeasing the mob scumbags who run this fkn business?"

Gil: "I'm not talking about the industry, just the quality of your recording. It's not working. This is going to take a lot longer in the studio than you're willing to put in..."

Immanuel: "Ed...,why do you talk like you know anything about tracking? I saw him vary the click; it was 89 on the verses and 106 on the chorus. He's making me fail to squeeze recording hours out of me, a total fkn scam! "

Ed: "Immanuel, this is the fourth producer I've dragged you to, and there's always something wrong..."

Immanuel: "... Yeah..., and there's always some shit going on that prevents me from getting a good mix down. None of them have the skills to master anything with a professional sound."

Ed: "You're trying to wear too many hats."

Gilberto: "Okay, that's it! Get the fck out of my studio. Both of you!"

Ed: "Now look what you've done! I'm out of options, Apollo; you just blew a great opportunity! He's got platinum all over his walls if you haven't noticed!"

Immanuel: "This is bullshit! Total hype! He has no ear and all he cares about is money. I'm outta here! He's a loser... "

Gilberto: "Ha..., you think anyone in this business is gonna tolerate your attitude.? Wait, you'll see, especially since you've got nothing to back it up! You're out of your mind... I was doing you, and Ed, a favor..."

Immanuel: "Ed's a fkn antique! Completely out of the sound loop."

Ed: "You're way out of line, here, sonny..."

Immanuel packs up his guitar and music and slams the door on his way out.

Eleven

A few days later Aimee is at the big party in Southampton with Roger. Immanuel is there picking up other women and flirting while her back is turned.

Jennifer Rydell: "I'm so excited about your work with animals. I've always believed they had souls, just look in their eyes. It's the proof we've been waiting for. I'd like to produce a documentary about your discovery."

Aimee: "Oh..., that would be wonderful!"

Jennifer: "But it's not going to be easy. It will definitely upset a lot of people on the other side of the issue. It'll force them to change the way they treat, and think about, animals!"

Roger walks over to escort Aimee to another room where he has arranged for her to meet a Movie Producer who is shopping for soundtrack composers. Roger enthusiastically introduces Aimee to the group of successful industry insiders, as they discuss ways to enhance story-telling in the age of special effects.

Roger: "Aimee, come, I want you to perform for Jack Deller, he's CEO of Brandaloro Studios..."

Immanuel has gathered a crowd of women who appear very impressed with him.

Aimee: "But Immanuel is a much better songwriter than I am..."

Roger: "Don't worry about him; he'll keep busy..."

Roger looks over his shoulder and sees women typing Immanuel's number into their smartphones. Aimee looks back towards him unaware of what's going on, but is quickly escorted away to a private room by Roger. Immanuel notices but continues flirting, networking, eating and feeding the women. One woman, Diana, is especially entertained.

A few minutes later, Aimee leaves the room with Roger happy and smiling, having been signed to a soundtrack deal. As they return to the gathering, Immanuel sees and comes over to her. Roger glares at Immanuel as he kisses Aimee, but then he walks away to seek out other business promotions.

Immanuel: "How'd it go? Did you get me the contract?"

Aimee: "Oh..., I'm so sorry. I really tried but I couldn't; he wouldn't let me promote you."

Immanuel: "But you got one, didn't you?"

Immanuel flies into a rage.

Immanuel: "See, I always knew he was an A-hole. Who the fckn hell is he to invade my affairs anyway?"

He grabs his guitar and goes toward the room to confront Roger when Aimee grabs his arm to stop him.

Aimee: "No..., don't! Please..., it'll create a problem..."

Immanuel: "No? You know what the problem is? YOU! All you care about is promoting yourself while you step on me! I'm just a tool for your wild ambitions. You don't know how to be a woman to a man like me! Don't look for me, I'm outta here!"

He looks at his phone as a call comes in, and leaves. Aimee gets very upset and runs after him, he shoves her away.

Aimee: "Immanuel, please don't leave... It's not my fault. I told Roger you're much better than me."

He briskly walks out the door, slams it, and hops into Diana's red sports car. They drive off as Aimee watches in tears. She goes back to the party upset and dejected, walks over to Roger shaken up and crying.

Diana is an ex-porn star bombshell who is now interested in producing and directing "women's porn." She is thinking of Immanuel as a new prospect as a porn star. She uses the time to solicit and seduce him to be in her movies.

Immanuel: "More than charming, let the night begin! Never thought I'd be whisked away by a savior that looks like you, Hot Wheels. You're a stick of dynamite!"

Diana: "Thanks. You're hot too. But we need to talk business. I produce and direct women's porn for exclusive web distribution. Pays very well."

Immanuel: "Haven't considered that market for my music since I don't watch porn. But okay... lay it on me..."

She suddenly swerves the car to the side of the road and pounces on him. They have quick, crazy sex in the car, steaming up the windows, bouncing and rocking the vehicle as cars drive by. When she's finished, she falls back into her seat and continues talking.

Diana: "I always tell my actors, just pleasure yourself like it's the last time you'll ever have sex. The rest comes natural and easy."

Immanuel: "You want me do THIS... on camera? Not used to an audience..."

Diana: "Just pretend you don't know there's a camera in the room..., like you just did..."

Immanuel: "Huh?"

She takes out a spy camera and shows him she recorded their affair. They both laugh.

Twelve

The following day Aimee is alone and crying. All of Immanuel's things are gone. She keeps calling him but he doesn't answer her. So she calls Clara to come over. Until she arrives, Aimee keeps replaying a message he left saying: *"Don't become a psycho-stalker, woman; I've moved on, now so should you!"*

Clara: "Hey, there..., you okay?"

Aimee shakes her head: "no." Clara brought over the video she shot of Immanuel and his tryst with Eleanor. She offers to show it to Aimee.

Clara: "Humn... I don't know..., maybe this isn't the best time to look at this..."

Aimee: "What is it?"

Clara: "I shot some video of Immanuel the night of your gallery show... Are you sure you should see this now?"

Aimee nods her head, "yes," so Clara shows Aimee the tape of the open mic scene, from when he picked Eleanor up at the bar, then went home to the studio for sex, later leaving with a vile confrontation.

Clara: "I can prove he's a total player, I know where he's going to be later. Come down..."

Aimee finds Immanuel at a bar drooling in the front row over **Clara who is performing** seductively with her electric guitar. She goes in to convince him to come back to her, seeing how Clara hooked him.

Aimee: "I'm really sorry I hurt you. Please forgive me and come home."

Immanuel: "Don't grovel; guys hate that! It was a mistake with you; I need a woman on my level, who understands what a man needs! This is Clara, my super hot, sexy lioness! Such awesome talent! I'm with her now."

He pulls Clara down onto his lap, kisses her, growls, squeezes her, then looks mockingly back at Aimee who runs home crying.

On Aimee's trip home, she trips and falls to the curb. A saxophone player appears out of the shadows, steps over and slowly nudges her back up like a tree come to life as an instrument. Hysterical, she struggles to walk on until falling a second time. A violinist passes with a sweet song lifting her with his bow. Soon after, she falls a third time, brokenhearted in tears, as an accordion player strolls by. Then a man comes along, lifts her up and escorts her home.

Thirteen

Immanuel spent a few weeks searching for his family online. He found a geneologist, Brice Jones, and made an appointment to consult with him. Then he meets with the ancestry researcher at his office.

Brice Jones: "So.., your name was changed to Immanuel Apollo? From what?"

Immanuel: "I never really had a name. Raised in foster care, I was called by whatever surname the new parents had. Every time I was reassigned, the host family renamed me."

Brice: "Do you have a certified copy of your birth certificate?"

Immanuel shakes his head, and says: "No."

Brice: "What do you know about your natural parents or nation of origin? Anything?"

Immanuel: "Nothing at all."

Brice: "That will make things difficult but not impossible. I'll need some time to trace back all of the homes you've been through, school reports, medical records, any living relatives..."

Immanuel: "How long will that take?"

Brice: "It's hard to say..."

Immanuel: "Look, I have to get an answer in three weeks."

Brice: "That may be an unrealistic expectation considering the lack of information provided. May I ask why after so long you have to find out so fast?"

Immanuel: "I have a pending record deal with a deadline."

Brice: "Sorry..., I don't see the connection..?"

Immanuel: "I've gotta find out who I am and where I came from, because I write soul songs, yet I can't sing my own. They want it."

Brice: "Interesting... what's a soul song?"

Immanuel: "When people get lost, I remind them of who they are, and what they're supposed to do with their lives. Freaky talent, I know..."

Brice: "Huh..., cool. I wonder..., have you ever heard of the Melimbe tribe? They're a remote sub-group within the Bembe's of Zambia?"

Immanuel: "I don't know anything about them. Why?"

Brice: "Did any of your foster families spend time in Zambia, or were any of African origin?"

Immanuel: "Not that I know of, they were all American."

Brice: "Alright, but I have a hunch about something. I'll give you a call in a few days..."

Immanuel leaves Brice's office and while he walks away in deep thought, Ed calls for a sudden meeting with Steve.

Ed: "The way we left off at Gilberto's really left a bad taste in my mouth for you, Immanuel. That was a very bad display. You got anything to say for yourself?"

Immanuel: "Yeah, why are you calling?"

Ed: "You know..., I shouldn't even tell you..., but Landau called for an early meeting. Could be he's changed his mind."

Immanuel: "I doubt it; more false hopes. I haven't met any of his criteria."

Ed: "Why be so negative? We won't know until we're in his office, so keep the fretting to the neck of your guitar."

They meet up at Landau's office. When they walk in another musician is being taken to Steve. Ed tells the receptionist they have an appointment. Then Immanuel and Ed are also escorted to Steve's office.

Steve: "Hey, glad you came down. I want you to hear one of the new artists I've signed; get a feel for someone with a marketable sound and style."

Jeremiah: "Yeah, thanks, Steve. Appreciate your support. Cool Man. Nice to meet you."

Steve: "His new single: "A Day In The Life" sold six digits the first week of release. It's why we went with Jeremiah instead of you. He's hot, young talent."

It's the same tune of the soul song Immanuel sang to Steve who secretly recorded it and passed it on to Jeremiah. The lyrics and melody are very similar too. Immanuel threatens a lawsuit.

Immanuel: "You soulless fkn bastard! You outright stole my original song!"

Steve: "Prove it! I told you it was common and I heard it before..."

Jeremiah: "Whoa, Steve..., I don't want to steal another artist's song..."

Steve: "Artist? He's a class A bullshit artist, nothing more! Don't worry, I'll handle it."

Steve calms Jeremiah down while Immanuel gets furious and storms out of the meeting. Ed follows.

Immanuel: "You summoned me here to tell me that? You sick fck!"

Ed: "Immanuel..., don't quit. I've got other contacts... I know people..."

Immanuel: "Screw yourself, old fool, you're not wasting any more of my time! Either you're a total dumbass, or you set me up for that!"

Ed chases him, then stands there catching his breath, holding his chest.

Ed: "No way..., I'm as shocked as you are!"

Immanuel: "Leech! I know what you did!"

ourteen

Immanuel arrives home angry, kicking stuff around his apartment. He takes out his computer and looks up the other musician's name while murmuring.

Immanuel: "Landau signed that boy toy over me? That guy's not worth shit! His music sucks! That's why he stole mine!"

He finds the definition of that artist's name which angers him more.

Immanuel: "Let's see... Jeremiah means: God will elevate..." SHIT! DAMN IT! I should rid the world of them! You hear me! Fck you all!"

He flies into a rage, breaking stuff, tossing it around, tearing his whole life to shreds in poorly restrained fury. While he's hacking through his place, a voice message comes thru from Aimee.

Aimee: "Immanuel..., are you okay? I love you."

He puts it on speaker and listens first, then manifests his madness.

Aimee: "Hello, Immanuel..., I just wanted..."

Immanuel: "Wanted what? To feel some fire in your oven? Cure your Vitamin O deficiency? When was the last time you had an orgasm and squirmed from the burn?"

Aimee: "Every time I think of you... in my heart!"

Immanuel: "Cheap, meaningless talk! If you really love me, get your hot ass over here and fck the smokin' devil out of me... "

Aimee: "Lust has nothing to do with love!"

Immanuel: "What are you ragging about? I'm a man, you dopey, little bitch! Trying to fkn castrate me? You don't give a sick shit about me! You're just a tease hooking for an ego boost."

He shuts the phone and throws it aside, foams and shouts: "God..., I hate her!"

Immanuel falls back on his bed and cries in frustration. She calls again.

Immanuel: "Go away! I know what's going on, you're a crazy ass broad sent from the netherworld to torment me to death. Seriously, you're bipolar or some fkn disorder, really, you should get a psych to help you over your delusions. And please..., for mine and everybody's sake, take the damn drugs, don't be delinquent on your meds, trust me, you need them."

He cuts the call off, tosses the phone across the room, and leaves his apartment.

Immanuel walks across town to the office building of Steve Landau. He passes security, signing in as going to visit his office by appointment. He takes the elevator to the roof, tosses his cigarette, gets out, and sneaks up the stairs to the roof by disabling the alarm combination.

Immanuel stands on a rooftop looking over the City, smoking weed, feeling despondent, morose, pondering what to do about his circumstances and about Landau stealing his song. While he considers various manners of vengeance, Priestess Plentavo appears in a smoky haze.

Plentavo: "Decisions, decisions... if you can't go up, might as well go down!"

Immanuel: "You want me to jump?"

Plentavo: "A remedy... quicker than many!"

Immanuel: "Not into it..."

Plentavo: "But you failed! Tiny audience, no hit songs, no contracts, no sales! Who even knows your impotent name?"

Immanuel: "Doesn't matter; I have a plan..."

Plentavo: "Oh, how nice. Hope your plan includes deleting her from your mind, because she's showing up on my screen way too much. I told you to train her like a dog. Tie her up, make her jealous, flirt in front of her, seduce then reject her, promise her everything and give her nothing, tell her she doesn't satisfy you in bed, her body is ugly..., suggest having threesomes, foursomes... she's in my way... "

Immanuel: "What are you so concerned about someone I don't even think about?"

Plentavo: "You think about her constantly, you know you can't lie to me!"

Immanuel: "You're crazy!"

Plentavo: "You're crazy too... about me! Look at this..."

She says each line with a different emotion or none at all..., then rips off her clothes to reveal a skimpy, seductive outfit below the cloak. There is a black fire snake twisted around her.

Plentavo: "You're confused... she's a mirage, not at all what you thought she was! Poof! All gone!"

Immanuel: "I don't want her! Okay... I ended it. You have to get over this obsession... so we can proceed with what you promised me..."

Plentavo: "Humor me.., Hamlet! You want to be a music god and rule over the charts? You require punition ..., blacksnake boy!"

Immanuel: "What?"

Plentavo: "You heard me..., worship me..., or butcher me..., now is that question!"

As she speaks, her arms and legs morph into different musical instruments as she strikes out to bash him with them. Out of them come ribbons of musical notes and staves that tie him up in a web. She pelts him with notes and rhythms, beating him with vibrations and waves of music. He fights to break free. Each command changes her image. The first she appears as a Shakespearean character, the second as a mythical deity then as a violent devilish sex goddess. Then she pulls out a huge ornate laser-electric sword and starts swinging wildly at him.

Plentavo: "Sacrifices must be made. Success is costly."

She keeps chopping and slicing at him, while he runs from side to side.

Immanuel: "What do you want?"

Plentavo: "Since your heart is divided, I will cleave it in two and take the half that belongs to me."

Immanuel: "No, I'll find another way...!"

Plentavo:"'No' is not an option..!. You want out? The door is DOWN!"

She sends out tentacles made of platinum and gold **musical staves with notes** firing at him like bullets. She tries to rope his arms and legs and drag him to the ledge to throw him over.

While swinging her sword, she drops it, he picks it up. She sends CDs hurling at him like frisbees to decapitate and chop him up, he slices himself free. Then she disappears by morphing into a terrifying demonic creature and flies off on a music scroll, rolls up, and disappears.

Shaken, he recovers then gathers himself and leaves.

Fifteen

Aimee arrives at her studio, where she meets Plentavo, disguised as a fortune teller, sitting at a table set up on the sidewalk outside her door.

Plentavo: "The future's not looking so good, huh?"

Aimee: "Sorry, I was just thinking about a sad subject; didn't mean to dampen anybody's outlook with my downcast expression."

Plentavo: "You really don't need to be so considerate of others. Maybe that's your problem."

Aimee: "How so?"

Plentavo: "I see a man in your life, one who isn't worth all you're heaving for him."

Aimee: "How do you know?"

Plentavo: "It's my business to know that and a lot more... Trust me, he's just one of many fish in the sea of possibilities for you. And if he's under-performing in the love game, time to replace him with another player. One you can position more favorably in your life. You don't deserve this!"

Aimee: "I appreciate your concern for me, but this relationship is so much more complicated than that. Really..., there's a lot involved here."

Plentavo: "He's mind-fckng you! It's all in your imagination. There's nothing on his end. It's a Cinderella fantasy. He's just playing you when he's got nothing else to do. He's been trash talking you to other women. If you don't get out now, emotionally, he'll just leave you for dead..., or worse! You must get away while you can. Before something happens."

Aimee: "Wow, that's very negative. And you sound like you know him... Who are you?"

An ambulance goes blasting up the Avenue causing a taxicab to collide with an SUV, which hits a parked car and jumps the curb. Aimee, seeing the danger, dodges the accident by running up the block quickly.

When the vehicles come to rest and the police start arriving at the scene, she walks back and finds that the fortune teller and her table have disappeared. Though the accident struck right where Plentavo and Aimee were, there was no trace of the fortune teller or any mangled table. Yet it was impossible for her to have moved it and gotten away that quickly.

Aimee enters her door, perplexed and stunned at what just happened.

Meanwhile across Town, Immanuel arrives at an upscale restaurant for lunch, where he was invited to meet a porn actress named Sappho. When he arrives, she's sitting with the Director he encountered in the Hamptons, Diana. They greet each other with seductive kisses, then get right to business.

Sappho: "So what's wrong with being a porn star? It's served me well, as you can see."

Immanuel: "I'm a musician, not an actor. I can produce your soundtracks, but that's all I'd be interested in."

Diana: "I told you..., there's a ton of money in this. When you're done, cash in and start your own record label, build a studio, whatever you want. It's not meant as a career path; it's a rich daddy with deep pockets!"

Sappho: "Tell me you wouldn't do me right now, right here on this table, if you could? So what's the big deal? Same shit, except you get paid!"

Immanuel: "Thanks for the offer, but it's not my thing. If we can work out a deal for the music, I'll sign on if the money's good."

Diana: "Okay, we can talk about the music. Don't see why not..., but take the script too. Look it over, see what you think. May help you decide."

Immanuel takes the script reluctantly then fans through it curiously. His eyebrow raises, he sighs, then stands up to leave. Sappho and Diana wink at each other assuming he won't be able to resist the story and money offered for the role.

But not wanting to risk losing him, Sappho dives on him, right in the restaurant, French kisses him, licks his face and neck aggressively, sucks on his neck leaving a bruise, and gropes his crotch as customers are dining. Diana giggles. Immanuel is surprised but reluctantly pushes her away, as she tries to push him down on the table and remove his shirt.

Shortly after he leaves the restaurant, he runs into Hortense, who has been stalking him. She wants her money back, but being obsessed with him, she also wants sex. She gets out of a waiting taxi.

Hortense: "Immanuel, over here... you know when we left the dungeon of Priestess Plentavo, I gave you a lot of money. It was to produce your CD. Why don't I have one yet?"

Immanuel: "Because I need another 20K to master it!"

She escorts him into the courtyard of a local park where they sit down to talk.

Hortense: "Si? Only one way you'll get that!"

She touches him seductively and changes her voice to a deeper, more sultry tone, exaggerating her Latin accent...

Hortense: "How come you don't give me sex? You give everybody else..."

Immanuel: "Call me prudish, but I don't mix business with pleasure."

Hortense: "That's bullshit! I think it's because I intimidate you! Too much woman!"

Immanuel: "Okay, Hortense..., to be real, I'd rather have my boys hacked off and fed to a fat rat!"

Hortense: "Why? Tell me why you say that! I don't believe you. I'm mucho-mucho sexy! You must think about me..., what it would be like..."

Immanuel: "No way! You spook me! There's an intense Lilith vibe about you..., you know, blood, gory shit, violence, cannibalism..., not into it!"

Hortense: "Fine then..., we'll consider this a business meeting. But I hope you will at least respect my tradition: I always 'salute' success, do you mind?"

She opens a bottle of wine, pours two plastic cups, and she lifts her cup to his, touching cups.

Hortense: "It's vintage.., tingles the tongue..."

Immanuel: "It's a good one, but it won't make me change my mind... One thing I'm not, and that's proof positive, I'm nobody's whore!"

She spills her drink in a staged accident, while he drinks his. She pours another cup for herself and puts it aside pretending she'll drink it, while they talk.

Hortense: "Hate to waste this stuff... Nobody carries it..., and for good reason..."

The poison begins taking effect... She gets up aggressively, he looks at his cup, starting to feel sick.

Hortense: "So, Mr. Business-scam... where's my return on investment?"

Immanuel: "Damn..., what the hell..., I feel weird... did you put something in this wine?"

She kicks him off the bench then spits on him and leaves. He struggles, shakes, sweats, then pukes repeatedly, scrapes himself off the ground, tries to get up and walk home, but keeps stumbling and vomiting along the way...

Meanwhile Aimee is sitting in her loft, staring out the window, sad about Immanuel and wondering where he is. While in deep thought about him, she becomes nauseous, gets a cramp, gags, and holds her stomach about to throw up.

Sixteen

A few days later Immanuel is on set in a NYC apartment ready to make the porn movie. Gazing out the window, he sees a toddler playing by a north-facing window across the street, about to fall out. He sees the danger, runs down the stairs and out into the street, just in time to catch the child and save her. The parents and neighbors run to thank him They hold onto him, as neighbors and other family members run to comfort the baby girl. They grab and hug him in appreciation, but he soon separates and leaves.

He goes back to the apartment and returns to the set of the film.

Diana: "This is Gigi Hancock. You'll be co-starring with her. As you've read, it's a simple story. Boy meets girl. Boy seduces girl. Girl teases boy. Boy takes girl aggressively. Boy reaches ecstasy. Girl is overwhelmed. Boy rejects Girl. And so on..."

Immanuel: "How does it end? What happens to the girl?"

Diana: "We'll see. That's up to you."

As Immanuel laments that his life has come to this, his phone rings. He looks to see who is calling, recognizes the number, and picks up.

Immanuel: "Hey Brice, what's up?"

Brice: "I'm leaving for three-weeks vacation tomorrow. We have to talk before I go."

Immanuel: "Stay there..., I'm on the way."

Immanuel, eager to redeem himself, bolts off the film set without explanation, runs downstairs, grabs a taxi, and races over to Brice's office.

As he bursts into the office, Brice hears and eagerly comes out to greet him.

Brice: "Hey, Immanuel... Wait till you hear what I've got."

Immanuel: "You found my family?"

Brice: "I did, and you've got quite a story.... To begin, you are: Jesse Michael Samson McFarland."

They walk back to the office together.

Immanuel: "That's who I am? Whoa, I've got to know what it means! A man's name is the title of his song."

Brice: "Somehow I knew you'd ask, so I checked it out... You are, in a sentence: "The Lord God is, and who is like our God, saith the man of the Sun, with the Spirit of the waves."

Immanuel: "Shit! All that corny God crap..., fck, it can't be me! Dude, you screwed up!"

Brice: "Nope, it's you! No doubt! I secured solid documentation."

Immanuel listens, but is confused.

Brice: Now about your parents: your father, Jonathan McFarland and mother, Rebecca Joubert, were both born in Cape Town, South Africa."

Immanuel sits back in the chair as Brice tells him about his birth family. His thoughts flash scenes of his childhood and life thereafter.

Brice: "They were well known and much loved medical missionaries who lived and worked in Zambia caring for the persecuted Melimbe people who suffered a lot of hardship, war, and ill health."

Hearing this Immanuel gets excited.

Immanuel: "Wow! Awesome! You must really dig your job! What's the contact info for my parents?"

Brice: "Unfortunately, the records also show that John and Bekha were killed in a tribal war before your first birthday. Your little sister, Emily, did not survive. The details regarding her cause of death were sketchy. You were brought to America by an Aid worker who knew your family. Since Emily was killed, he was afraid you might be too."

Immanuel slumps into his chair with a sense of great despair flooding over him.

Immanuel: "Savage bastards! You sure this is real?"

Brice: "Unfortunately, I always regret having to deliver information like this, but it's accurate, or I'd be in loads of trouble for passing it on... May I continue?"

Immanuel: "Guess it can't get any worse... Yeah..., go ahead, let's hear the rest ..."

Brice: "You were never formally adopted by your American foster families due to an unresolved citizenship dispute with the Government of Zambia resulting from a non-traditional belief the tribe held about you. That's all I could access."

Immanuel: "But this doesn't resolve anything for me. It's more of a tease than an appeasement. I need more information..."

Brice: "I understand..., but you'll have to go to Africa to find it. And plan to stay a while; there's no way to estimate how long the discovery process might take. I have an associate, an Anthropologist, Dr. Alison Denton, working the field there. She's very familiar with the Melimbens, and she's spent many years with them. If there are any survivors who knew your parents, she'd be the one to know."

Immanuel: "Look, I'll go! Just make all the arrangements. You cool with that?"

Brice: "Sure will, send her an email tonight."

Immanuel stands in a restrained state of shock, fixes his hair, shakes hands with Brice and leaves the office thinking of the uncertainty ahead in his quest.

When Immanuel arrives home, he takes out his guitar and writes a song to express his mixed feelings: **"Can't Find Myself"**.

Seventeen

Immanuel is on his way to the airport to catch his Zambian flight. He waves to hail a taxi, but no cabs stop for him. A black limo slowly slips up to the curb where he is standing, like a shark sneaking up on its prey. The rear passenger door of the limo opens and a sexy woman, Delilah, sitting in the back seat, says:

Delilah: "I hate to see a sexy guy unable to get a cab. Hop in.... Hi, I'm Delilah. Where you going? I'm on the way to Kennedy..."

Immanuel: "Nice, rescued by a bombshell... Can you drop me at Air Africa."

Delilah : "Sure...! Big trip.... for a big..., man!"

He gets into the back seat with her. As they drive toward the airport, she pulls a curtain across the back glass partition, blocking the view of the driver. Then she begins to seduce him, kisses him, rips his clothes off, and has wild sex with him on the bottom to keep him from seeing where he's going.

Delilah: "You're so hot, let's not rush this..."

117

Immanuel: " Oooph, nice boobs, those real? Ass too! Incredible! Let's see what other big boys toys you got? Come on, open wide for the doctor... , Oooh baby, I'm all yours, until these wheels stop."

Delilah: "That's all? Only until we get to the airport? Don't you want to keep in touch?"

She massages him all over...

Immanuel: "Probably not. Nice as you are... I've got a woman I plan to marry."

She laughs and prods him in a teasing way.

Delilah: "You sick beast! What would she say if she saw you now?"

Immanuel: "You're a bitch! ... I'm a man... She knows that. It comes with the territory!"

Delilah: "Oh yeah? You know what I say about that?"

The car hooks a sharp turn and slows down.

Immanuel: "I don't know, Baby, why don't you tell me?"

Delilah: "A real man can't just give it..., he also has to be able to take it!"

Immanuel: "Okay, on your back, I'll take ya!"

Suddenly the car speeds up, then screeches to a halt. The doors fling open. The Driver is joined by three other armed men who order him out of the car, while she sits back, gets dressed and giggles, lights a cigarette and blows the smoke at him. One of the men tells her: "Stay here" She was used as a decoy to lure him. They tear off a bunch of bills and throw them at her in the car. She gathers them up. They drag him out along the ground half-dressed as he struggles to stand up. They roughly escort him into an abandoned industrial building where Roger and Mike await.

Immanuel: "Damn! You set me up! Who the hell are they?"

Orlaf: "Shut the fk up! Just make it worse..."

Driver: "Pleasure and pain, you must know they go together like vodka and caviar."

They drag him through a chained door into an abandoned warehouse where Roger and Mike wait under candlelight. They throw him into a broken chair and tie him up.

Roger: "Humn... Recognize me now? Roger Falcone! Husband of Leann! Capice?"

Immanuel: "No, Guido. I don't know you or your wife; and I've got a plane to catch..."

Mike: "What? No respect? Go for it!"

Guiccomo: "The only thing you're going to catch is a fatal beating."

Orlaf: "Right way to finish an unworthy life."

Guiccomo and Orlaf punch, kick, slap, and spit on him, also tear chunks of his hair out.

Mike: "They're right. Now's not the time to play the wiseass card."

Roger: "You know what you did to her and to me. It's time you came down for sentencing."

Immanuel: "So I fkd your dead wife! Yeah..., and she told me everything! Too fkn bad, get over it!"

Roger nods and the henchmen beat him again.

Roger: "That's right, you evil, heartless prick! Guess what it feels like on the receiving end?"

Roger gives the okay for them kick him in the stomach, he gasps for air. His face is cut and bloody while his hair is singed with a cigarette lighter.

Immanuel: "Kill me, go ahead! The Feds were on my butt for a parole violation...; they may already have the building surrounded...."

Mike: "Eh, we ain't worried."

Immanuel: "Okay..., since you brought it up..., ever wonder why she was so vulnerable to me?"

Mike: "Didn't Momma teach you it's bad manners to discuss, politics, religion, and sex with other men's wives?"

Roger smacks him personally.

Mike: "Disrespect, I told you, don't do it!"

Immanuel: "She shot herself over you..., your obsession with Aimee! And now, I'm a victim of that obsession myself! Leann didn't give a shit about me! She used me to fill the emptiness you left in her soul. Go ahead, '86' me, but it won't rid you of the guilt!"

Roger gets enraged, and is just about to kill Immanuel when noise is heard outside. Two Security Guards on night patrol, enter the building with flashlights. The men split, leaving Immanuel inside.

He wriggles out of the ropes and staggers off quietly into the night, bloody and battered.

He texts Aimee saying he loves her and is sorry how badly he treated her, and knows she's the only woman who ever truly loved him, but that he has to find himself and is going overseas for an indefinite period of time. Not sure when or if he'll return. However, his phone battery dies and the text does not transmit; she never gets it.

# Eighteen

Aimee sits down to write a love poem to Immanuel. She plans to send it off as an email, though she does not know that he has left the Country and will be away for an indefinite period of time.

She struggles with inspiration to breathe the first poetic verse, typing several then deleting them. She looks out at the sky when two doves land on her windowsill. The birds engage each other in courting behavior by singing, preening each other, tweeting, snuggling up close, feeding each other, and cooing.

While observing the two loving birds, the inspiration comes.

"Immanuel, you are the only one I love,
My songbird, soul mate, my heroic dove.
All my life I waited for you to appear,
But then you flew away because of fear."

As she writes, her sensitivity intensifies...

"I feel like I can't breathe without you,
The sky seems dim and no longer blue.
My dreams are empty, my future bleak,
Because I cannot feed you from my beak."

The birds begin mating on the ledge...

"I no longer feel your scratch under my feathers,
Or have your help to untie my daily tethers.
While my vivid colors grew so deep in tone,
You saw them all yet still left me alone."

Just then, the male bird flutters his wings and flies away... She cries hard.

"I felt such pain while you pursued other birds,
As I remembered each of your loving words.
I was sculpted as your perfect mate,
Both watchers of time and bloomers of late."

The female starts to chirp, calling the male.

"How I long to build your tender nest,
Where you can lay your head upon my breast.
And shield each other from life's pounding rains,
As we greet each day that on Earth remains."

Another bird lands a few feet away, she waddles away from him, then he flies off.

"I miss my lovebird cooing in the misty night,
The morning joys we shared in dreamy flight.
And our young chicks that we shall never see,
Unless by the seven graces you return home to me..."

Just as she clicks 'send' the male returns.

Outside the warehouse, Immanuel staggers to the water not knowing where he is. It's early sunrise and he's missed his plane. He staggers to the dock where an impressive ship, with sails and engines, has pulled in for fuel and prep. He meets the mariners, two brave men sailing the seven seas.

Immanuel: "Hey Man..., I had a hard night, missed my damn flight. Can you get me outta here? I've got a few bucks..."

Emett Harding: "Sure mate, climb on deck. We'll be ready to sail out in about fifteen minutes."

They look at Immanuel and see he's badly beat up.

Isamu Reynard: "Looks like that hard night left its mark. Think you need medical attention?"

Immanuel: "Nah, I'm alright."

Emett: "They may not let you board a plane like that."

Immanuel: "How'd you guys know I was going to the airport?"

Isamu: "Just a hunch... You can clean up in the cabin. There's first aid in the back closet."

Immanuel goes down into the cabin, bandages, and tends to himself while the guys prep the ship for sail. He looks around amazed at the abundance of the vessel, how well supplied and built it is, then returns to deck preparing for the journey.

Immanuel: "Looks like you're prepared for anything and everything..."

Isamu: "Wisdom requires it. The deep is a restless teacher, especially to reluctant students."

Emett: "Where are you trying to go?"

Immanuel: "Ha..., Zambia..., in Africa. And you?"

Emett: "A port in Madagascar. Want a ride?"

Immanuel: "No shit? How long will it take?"

Emett: "Last time we were out for about five months. Can you be away from the world that long?"

Isamu: "A lengthy stretch at sea can change a man."

Immanuel: "Sounds like good medicine. I'm in..."

Emett: "Then come on..., let's set these sails."

Energized and inspired, they finish prepping, then set sail into the sunrise together as a fresh, new skyscape streaks itself before them.

Immanuel hears a new song starting to play in his head, but he can't quite catch it... Intuitively, he knows it's his soul song, but he's too excited to take hold of it. Every time he tries to stop it and remember the parts, it slips away... But he knows the name of it: "**Shadow Of The Light Man**".

# Nineteen

The next evening, Aimee and Dalisay are about to present their research findings at a packed colloquium.

University Chair: "Welcome to our quarterly symposium. This marks the first presentation to the scientific community in this controversial field of study. A question and answer session will follow the discussion, so without any further delay, here are: Dr. Aimee Lucina and research associate, Dr. Dalisay Corazon."

The audience applauds but reluctantly and sparsely. The technician lowers the screen and turns on the overhead computer presentation for everyone to see. Aimee is about to speak when the Technician running the computer shouts out with urgency.

Technician: "Hold up..., there's a problem with this program. The data appears to either be encrypted or scrambled. Do you have a code or a backup file?"

Aimee: "That's bizarre, it should be clear."

Dalisay: "I have a copy; I'll send it over."

Dalisay runs off the stage toward the building where the research lab and her office is. When she gets there, she sees that her computer is missing and her office has been ransacked. She immediately calls Aimee.

Dalisay: "My computer's gone, somebody robbed my freakin' office. I can't believe this! Do you have another copy on your hard drive?"

Aimee: "Oh God! This could be disastrous! I do have a copy in my office, but don't go alone."

Dalisay: "It's okay, people are still working. Tell me where to look..."

Dalisay talks on the cell to Aimee while she runs to her office. She gets to the office and sees that it's been ripped apart and robbed. She exclaims in shock.

Dalisay: "What the...? Shit! Who did this? And why?"

She notices that one security camera was left untouched.

Dalisay: "The camera's there! Looks like it's working... Hector...? Where's that guard...?"

She turns to leave the office to find Hector, the guard, and bumps into Robert in the doorway.

130

Robert: "Who's on the phone? Who are you talking to?"

Dalisay: "It's Aimee."

Robert: "Ah-ha... Hang up."

Dalisay: "I'll call you back."

She puts her phone down in Aimee's office but deliberately does not disconnect the call.

Dalisay: "I'm so glad you're here. Look at this! By chance, did you see anyone?"

Robert: "Of course not, I was in the Lab. Now you've got me worried! My office better be the way I left it..."

The audience is becoming impatient and irate calling out to get things underway.

Aimee: "While observing the fertilization of.."

Bruce: "We've already reviewed your claim, that science has proven 'living beings have souls', which combust into life as you've coined it: "a fire song" and that you've observed the genesis of such?"

Elliott: "Right. So we're not here for you to expound upon religious assumptions, but to see the actual experiments and data you allegedly have."

Terrence: "Frankly, the whole notion you propose is patently unscientific..., and essentially useless. Even if there was a shred of truth in your theory, and it is at best, only an unsubstantiated theory,where are the applications for it?"

Every time Aimee attempts to address their skeptical retorts, another audience member shouts out a critical comment.

Meanwhile Dalisay has found security and is showing them the two offices. Hector calls the police. When they go back to Aimee's office, Dalisay notices that the camera, which was intact, is now missing.

Dalisay: "The camera's gone! It was here before..., undisturbed. I looked right at it!"

Security looks at her suspiciously until Robert comes around the corner out of breath and upset.

Robert: "They got me too. Looks like a cyclone ripped through town. Call the police!"

Hector: "I did; they're on the way."

Robert: "Where were you when all of this was going down? Why do we pay for security if this is the kind of service you provide?"

Back in the auditorium Aimee continues to apologize.

Aimee: "We're still having a technical glitch."

She looks over at the technician who shrugs that no help is on the way.

Leon: "I think we've given this about all the time it merits."

Leon gets up to leave; everyone else gradually follows until the room is empty.

The Police have arrived at the Lab, they look over the crime scenes, and take the testimonies of Dalisay, Robert, Hector, and a maintenance worker. Then they leave along with the guards. Robert shuts the light and leaves along with a maintenance worker. Dalisay closes the door to her office once more when she remembers her phone was left in Aimee's office. So she goes to get it.

On the way there, she sings aloud through the hallway, a spontaneous song: **A Better Place.** She looks for it in the spot she left it, but it's not there. Just then she hears a robotic voice in the doorway. She turns around and sees a person in black wearing a hooded mask holding up her phone.

Masked Person: "Looking for this?"

Startled, she freezes and gasps as the light is shut. Dalisay tries to escape but is grabbed. Trying to fight back, she shouts for help as she is strangled.

One of the researchers returns from hanging out in a bar after dinner with friends. He discovers Dalisay dead on the floor. He checks her vital signs, then calls the police and an ambulance.

Aimee arrives when Dalisay's body is being taken out on a stretcher, covered up. Lights flashing from the emergency vehicles and news trucks there illuminate spectators standing around. The scene is cordoned off. Strolling pedestrians stop to eavesdrop and gather information as the police officers interview Aimee, who is extremely upset and wiping tears from her eyes.

Police Office Thompson: "Do you have any idea who might have wanted to hurt her? Terminated employees? Failed students? Ex-boyfriends?"

Aimee: "No, nobody... she was amazing! Everyone loved her. Dalisay was my right hand..."

Police Office McNamara: "When was the last time you saw Dr. Corazon?"

Aimee: "She left the auditorium about two hours ago."

Thompson: "Do you know why she walked out? Or where she was going?"

McNamara: "Right..., also where were you? And what were you doing during that time?"

Twenty

About one month has passed. Immanuel rises early and plays guitar with Isamu as they sit at the back of the boat looking at the sky.

Immanuel: "Interesting how the ocean reflects the sky."

Isamu: "Yes..., hard to say which one is more mysterious..."

Immanuel: "Tell me about it..., my whole life is shrouded in mystery... Ever have something so elusive that you couldn't find it no matter where you looked?"

Isamu: "Reminds me of the saying: 'You can search the whole world and still never find, for the man in the mirror, will to himself, always be blind."

Immanuel is surprised that Isamu intuitively knew what he was referring to.

Immanuel: "Yeah... *sigh* ... This salty air's addictive. I can see myself getting hooked on it!"

Isamu: "Ha..., like I did..., on the beach in Tahiti... spellbound by the glowing, turquoise surf...."

As Isamu tells his story, Immanuel enters into a daydream state and vividly recounts all that is being told to him as if he had also been there. A fat, middle-aged man in a bikini, a young girl afraid of water, a handicapped man in a wheelchair, young guys with surfboards, a group of teenage girls, an old woman, an enthusiastic toddler with his dad, several families, and dogs, all walking down the beach and going into the ocean ...

Isamu: "Then I watched as an amazing thing happened..., a succession of docile waves processed ashore and floated everyone into its buoyancy. While the air fizzled up in a kind of misty effervescence, time appeared to dissolve into eternity. All of the differences that divide people and every other creature were washed away by the Great Equalizer. There was this joyful, sparkling oneness I'll never forget..."

Immanuel: "Yeah..., I get that!'"

Isamu: "But it's not always that way, the tides can turn to become an impartial judge."

Immanuel: "What makes it go one way or the other?"

Isamu: "Depends where you are in the song."

Immanuel: "Song? Ha..., what do you mean?"

Isamu: "Music vibrates throughout the cosmos and nature's teeming with it. Even the brain composes and performs 24/7..., while the bodies of every living thing respond to the various types of music. Some can make you well, other kinds can make you sick. The ocean is especially rich with rhythm and melody. A lot of storytelling going on down there... ever try playing with it?"

Isamu walks away leaving Immanuel curious and intrigued by the challenge. He starts playing his guitar to the rhythm and sounds of the ocean, sky, and birds flying overhead.

Seabirds sing and chirp and he replies. Then more birds hover and land on the boat, enjoying the music, they sing together before flying away. He's amazed, looks around for the guys, but they are elsewhere.

He alone witnesses these wonders. A group of happy dolphins swim up to the ship. They porpoise, sing, and talk to him. Then with a grand show, they swim around the boat, wave at him, and swim off, as the flock of sea birds fly in formation overhead...

A pod of whales pass nearby making waves that give Immanuel a fun ride. Moments later, a lone Sperm whale approaches in a majestic display, while Isamu and Emett return to deck. Immanuel is jubilant like a young boy.

Immanuel: "Awesome, man! You wouldn't believe what just happened!"

Emett: "And... it's not over yet..., look who's coming..."

Isamu: "A Sperm whale, that's a rare sighting out here."

Immanuel: "Why's he heading toward us? We have to change course... he could overturn this boat!"

Emett: "Actually..., looks like he's cruising in for a visit."

Isamu: "Must have been your music; they love it... They're considered the virtuoso composers of the entire animal kingdom... Bet you didn't know that!"

Immanuel: "That is a new one!"

Emett: "Ah-ha, here he comes, get your guitar ready."

The whale comes right up and porpoises in front of them to announce his arrival. Then he comes alongside the vessel, waves, sings to them out of his blowhole, and smiles. Immanuel struggles to play a song back, note for note, turning the whale's melody into rhythmic chords. They do a duet together. Their energy and synergy increases until the whale turns around, porpoises again, and swims away.

Immanuel: "Damn! That dude rocked the house!"

Emett: "He did indeed!"

Isamu: "Sperm whales have the largest brains and capacities of all the toothed mammals; they also dive deeper than any other creature."

Immanuel: "Makes sense..., more intelligence, greater depth..."

Isamu: "And they don't only make music for mating purposes; but they also sing what I call, 'soul songs'. These are used to identify, validate, and direct individual whales within their pods. A lot of feeling is transferred through these songs. They're soulful and distinct, arising from deep within the animal..."

Immanuel: "Wow, whales sing soul songs too? Hey, Moby, where'd you get the gift?"

Back in the City Aimee is playing music with Clara up in the loft. It's now apparent that Aimee is pregnant. They stop jamming to talk.

Clara: "Glad you're eating again; looks like you've gained a little of your weight back. You had me worried for a while there..."

Aimee: "It's not fat...; I'm pregnant."

Clara: "Whoa girl..., or should I say..., you go girl! From who? Don't tell me, was it Roger?"

Aimee: "No. It was Immanuel."

Clara: "What? Wait up..., you told me you didn't have sex with him."

Aimee: "Right! That's true; I didn't!"

Clara: "Now you're spooking me! The birds and the bees, uh-huh, you know how that works."

Aimee: "The night we got naked together..., I must have gotten too close somehow... It's rare, but it happens occasionally."

Clara: "Dang, that guy's toting around the Olympic swim team on steroids..."

Aimee: "Maybe..., but I was also wearing Lily Of The Valley flower essence....I've used it a lot in fertility studies; it attracts and energizes them like crazy."

Clara: "Call me stupid..., but Huh? Oh, never mind, if you say so..."

Aimee: "Another thing this shows me.... we're definitely soul mates since something this uncommon must have been meant to be. There's a higher purpose at work here. Just wish I knew what it was..."

 **Twenty One**

Now about three months into the trip, Emett steps on deck to alert Immanuel and Isamu about some storms brewing over the ocean.

Immanuel: "It amazes me how colorful fish are! If you think about it, there's no light down there, who's going to see that spectacular panorama?"

Isamu: "You'll have to ask the brilliant Artist who painted them!"

Immanuel: "Who you talking about? Darwin? Ha-ha! Hope you're not one of those God nuts..."

Isamu: "Ha! Hope I am! Love cures insanity, it doesn't cause it. But infatuation, lust, jealousy..."

Immanuel: "Yeah, I know..., those are camels of a different hump..., ha!"

Emett: "We have to change course and head south. Three tropical depressions developed off the Sahara; two have already become hurricanes."

Immanuel: "Seriously? Are they tracking this way?"

Emett: "Appear to be. We must move quickly. It'll get rough out here. Secure yourself downstairs."

Immanuel: "How close are they? The wind's picking up..."

Emett: "The first one..., Jezebel, a Category 3, is moving quickly around a tight, well-formed eye, at about 8 knots, wind speeds between 65-87 knots, about 130 km away, checking longitude and latitude. We could be in her outer bands within an hour or so."

Immanuel: "Sounds like an event. You'll need my help; I'll go up with you."

Isamu: "You're not ready yet... But don't be afraid; you'll be okay. You see..., I know how and why you found yourself with us, and that your search isn't over yet..."

The bad weather suddenly intensifies and the storm announces itself with a strong, circular wind. It rocks the boat, almost tipping it.

Immanuel: "Whoa! Here it comes... Look, if anything happens, do you have family you want me to contact? You never did tell me where you come from..."

Isamu: "That doesn't matter now. But I have something I must leave with you. It's this... I know you won't understand this, but it's from your father."

Isamu places a gold medallion in Immanuel's hands with an unfamiliar family seal on it.

Immanuel: "You're too young to have known my father... What's this all about?"

Isamu: Stay focused on what you are to do for a little while longer... Remember, the meaning of life is love and the purpose of life is to spread His light."

Immanuel: "But how am I supposed to do this? I've always thought it was going to happen with my music. But now I'm confused. If I have some kind of personal mission, I have no clue what it is!"

Isamu: "You know! It's why you were given the power of music, as a weapon against evil. It can move the forces of the universe, and it touches the heart of the Lord of Song. Now have faith, Jesse, take up your sword, and fire on the enemy!"

Isamu goes down into the cabin, grabs hold of Immanuel's guitar and strongly hands it to him like a machine gun. Sparks shoot out of it. The storm and ocean become turbulent and the sky is turning black. Isamu shuts door and runs up to stand with Emett.

Immanuel paces around the cabin, looking out as the storm winds whip the ship, slamming it against waves, turning it around, rocking it from side to side, almost knocking it over, shaking it, breaking parts off.

On deck Emett and Isamu fight to keep the ship afloat as a huge twisting funnel comes and carries them both upward into the sky. They ascend with their arms outstretched like divers over a cliff, spiraling around up into the whirlwind. When they reach the clouds, they pass through a light portal and disappear.

Immanuel doesn't know what happened and that the ship is at sail without its captain. Filled with a burst of courage, he runs on deck to find that the boat is taking on water and heading straight into the hurricane.

As Isamu taught him, Immanuel fights against the winds and surf, by playing a spontaneous song: "**Love Can't Fail.**" He battles the storm fiercely until a waterspout forms and catches the vessel, spinning it like a top. He holds onto the rail while almost being thrown into the Sea. For the first time in his life, the reality of his own mortality is real to him.

Immanuel gets knocked out as his head bangs the side wall. He falls unconscious and enters into a spiritual state. Moments later, a giant Pistol Shrimp snaps his claws blasting a sonic boom that opens a supernatural curtain behind which he proceeds.

Through the murky waters, he sees the sperm whale that he sang with returning, calling him with the soul song they shared. He rides him through the ocean's depths into a hidden dimension to learn what music really is: the language of the soul. He is shown that melody represents feeling and rhythm represents action. The lyrical, expressive quality of music speaks the secret matters of the heart; while the tempo flows forth the vitality of the spirit. And this language is spoken by everything in nature, even from tree to tree.

He listens to the spirit of music teaching him secret truths with sounds and beats that are unfamiliar and curious. Then he hears Isamu's voice speaking to him. At first it was straining to distinguish, but then it became clear, though he could not be seen.

Isamu: "It is recorded that the universe was spoken into existence. But perhaps it was sung, then with great passion exploded into light. And from this love song, came all light; then from His light, came everything else. In this age of awe, scientists theorize that the first particles to appear in the earliest cosmos were photons. And if we follow the trail of first light backwards, we will find that the entire universe is God's soul song, as it came out of Him, and it continues to vibrate with the divine resonance."

Then Immanuel is taken to a deeper level and shown mysteries about life, music, and the soul that are so profound they cannot be translated into words. Some of the mysteries are familiar, like those about the Golden Curve, Fibonacci numbers, time itself as a circi-linear spiral, perfect repeating patterns found in nature, fractal kaleidoscopes of colored truth that reach beyond human comprehension, and the DNA helix as a ladder of lines and staves inscribed into which is every song of every life from the first to the last of days.

Immanuel is escorted at an accelerating rate of velocity into a brilliant light stream where he hears an ethereal piece of music that sounds hauntingly familiar, though he cannot identify it or figure it out. Somehow he senses it's about him, his song, but he can't comprehend it. He senses that it's his song but somehow emerging through someone else's song, but he can't identity who. He reaches the speed of sound and continues accelerating toward the speed of light. As he proceeds, afraid of dematerializing, he sees his future ahead, in a crystalline state, where the tube of light appears to reservoir into a pool of cobalt blue. He watches his future as if it was his past, and he sees himself burst through the speed of light into something quicker, another realm, but he doesn't know how or what the number was.

Suddenly he awakens as the clouds hastily rush away to their next assignment. He gathers himself, looks for Emett and Isamu everywhere and overboard, calls them, then sadly realizes they're lost. He goes up to try to figure out how to sail the ship. Miraculously, he's spun out the other side of the storm far away yet is completely intact.

Twenty Two

Robert uploads some new research data to his computer, then he calls an overseas colleague, Edgar Rhunhoffer, to boast and schedule himself at several upcoming symposiums.

Robert: "Dr. Rhunhoffer, please."

Edgar Rhunhoffer: "Hello."

Robert: "Edgar, good news! My research has concluded favorably! I'm ready to make my findings public. Will you have a spot for me at the Conference in Munich?"

Edgar: "Yes, of course... But have you really done it? Have you actually seen the soul?"

He switches to a hand-held phone, while he looks curiously out the window and sees a car pull up in front of his house. A plain clothes detective steps out and looks around, before slowly walking up to his front door.

Robert: "Not only have I seen it, but I've also created it."

Edgar: "Marvelous! Truly. Pure genius!"

Robert continues talking while looking out the window to see someone looking around his property.

Robert: "Ha! Ever think I would be the Nobel Laureate from our class? I must tour Europe first; the States lag behind on the innovation curve..."

Detective Grady rings the doorbell as Edgar explains the delay.

Edgar: "Ah-ha..., well the soonest symposium is scheduled for next season."

Robert: "Really? Three months? Look..., I've got the media at my door. I'll call you in a couple of weeks. Things are warming up, see what you can do."

Robert eagerly opens the door and greets the shield-brandishing Grady.

Robert: "No camera? Which news agency are you from?"

Grady: "Are you Robert Endicott Takatis? Detective Grady. I'm investigating the murder of your research colleague, Dr. Dalisay Corazon..."

Meanwhile Immanuel is on the boat trying to call for help, but can't get through to anyone, he's in a dead zone. Then the clouds break. The sun beams through as a blazing ray and falls on Emett's phone. A call begins to transmit to the Merchant Marines.

Immanuel: "Hello... I'm stranded off the coast of Africa somewhere. I've come through a hurricane and a waterspout. My crew fell overboard. They're gone, I looked everywhere, no sign... How far away is the nearest rescue vessel?"

The operator responds to him as another vessel comes into view. It appears to be moving towards him. Clouds pass overhead and the phone goes dead again. Haze in the distance clears to reveal land, and that he is within three miles of shore. The approaching vessel is still shrouded in fog.

Immanuel: "Hey..., over here, man..."

He whistles, yells out, and grabs binoculars to look, helping him see the ship and its crew clearly. He waves for help and calls out; but as the dense haze dissipates, it reveals he's befriending an armed enemy.

Immanuel: "Shit! It's a fkn rogue ship with armed pirates?"

A shot is fired and a shell passes him. He runs for cover in a confused panic. As soon as he hides, a gun battle erupts between the pirate ship and a rescue ship patrolling the open waters.

Back in the City, at the studio, Aimee is now visibly pregnant and having a baby room built for her twins. A decorator is going through various design options with her as the carpenters proceed with their woodwork. Sandy stands up and surveys the space.

Decorator Sandy: "What kind of a mood are you thinking here?"

Aimee: "Serenity and a love of nature."

Sandy: "I'd go with green then... it's a perfect color to provide that peaceful, natural vibe. Great for boys or girls. Do you know what you're having?"

Aimee: "Yes..., both. They're fraternal twins."

Sandy: "I envy you..., you got one of each and only had to get pregnant once!"

Aimee: "Yeah..., it's gotta be on their father's side; don't know of any twins in my tree..."

Sandy: "You know..., I really hope I don't offend you, but I've got to be honest here... you're such a talented artist, a beautiful woman, have a son and a daughter on the way, and you own this drop dead gorgeous loft in the coolest part of the City..., yet you seem very down to me. Is there anything you need to talk about? Decorating is a new profession for me; I didn't always do this..."

Aimee: "Oh? What did you do before?"

Sandy: "I was a professional networker."

Aimee: "What's that about?"

Sandy: "Meeting people..., everywhere! And in every kind of business, study, service professionals, creative pursuits, whatever..., and then connecting them to other people who needed what they had. I loved it!"

Aimee: "Then why'd you leave it?"

Sandy: "I still do it for friends, but it got to the point where I needed something more hands on, more personally creative where I could participate in the whole process of a project, from start to finish. In networking you rarely find out what the outcome of a connection is. I like decorating because I still get to meet a lot of cool people, such as yourself, and help configure their space for the maximum feng shui."

Aimee: "Nice!"

Sandy sees Aimee isn't responding with much energy and doesn't seem to feel like talking. It also appears she's struggling to handle hidden hurts and concerns. So she offers a contact of her own to help ease the burdens she's bearing. She blurts it out.

Sandy: "Myra has been amazing in my life. I wouldn't be here now if not for her! Seriously..."

Aimee: "Who's Myra?"

Sandy: "My personal life coach. But she's very different..., nothing like the others. She's truly gifted."

Aimee: "Yeah? How so?"

Sandy: "Her advice is unbelievable! It's like she knows everything, even stuff before it happens, and what people are really thinking and feeling."

Aimee: "Cool... has it helped you?"

Sandy: "Are you kidding? She totally saved my marriage, something nobody else could do. I tried everything before I consulted with her."

Aimee: "Really? How'd she do it?"

Sandy: "It's going to sound so simple it seems ridiculous..., but she said I should write my husband a letter explaining everything I couldn't get the chance to say because he wouldn't listen. And to make sure I don't hit him with any guilt or blame. Men hate that!"

Aimee: "Did it work?"

Sandy: "That's what I'm saying!"

Aimee: "Gosh! Why?"

Sandy: "Men can't figure us out. They want to come back, but don't because of the fear factor. An honest letter reassures them it's safe to try again."

Aimee: "What about a love poem?"

Sandy: "Nah, forget that. Men need it all laid out for them in plain terms. They get lost in metaphor, symbolism, and emotion. Especially about feelings, you've got to be real straight up with them or they'll get suspicious you're trying to manipulate them for something..."

Aimee: "Thanks for the insight."

Sandy: "Sure. Let me know what happens... I have another appointment today, so if we can, let's finish going over the decorating details for the room."

They complete the design choices and Sandy leaves. An hour later, the carpenters leave and Aimee sits down to compose the letter to Immanuel. As she begins, she cries again.

Detective Grady has gone to Roger's house and is discussing Dalisay's murder with him.

Grady: "I understand that Immanuel Apollo had some contact with Aimee and possibly also with Dr. Corazon. Do you know how I can reach him?"

Roger: "Last I heard he was booked on an overseas flight. No one's seen him around or got any calls, so I assume he made it out."

Grady: "What I'm in the dark about regarding this murder is what motive Immanuel may have had to eliminate Dalisay. Nothing obvious is emerging here... Is there any reason you can think of?"

Grady gets up and paces around the room.

Roger: "Trust me, I wouldn't have to dig too deep... he took over Aimee's loft and he cashed in on her new Art series; likely thought he'd profit on her research too. Corazon, as a business partner like me, was in the way. And I hear he's got a penchant for dead women, especially married ones."

Grady: "What about Aimee? Would she have wanted full credit?"

Roger: "Hell, no! Kill somebody? No chance! She won't even squash an insect, she puts them all outside. Religiously!"

Grady: "Anybody else?"

Roger: "No one I would know..."

Grady: "What about their lab associate, Dr. Takatis?"

Roger: "Robert? From what I understand he's an annoying whack job but they don't work together. A geeky pain in the butt, but otherwise harmless."

Twenty Three

The rescue ship that apprehended the pirates, deposits Immanuel on the shore in Angola, where he is picked up by Anthropologist Dr. Alison Denton who has been waiting for him. As he climbs down, he thanks his shipmates and calls out across the shore.

Immanuel: "Yeah, that's her. Thanks, Man..." "Dr. Denton?"

Alison: "I'm here..., Jesse! So wonderful to finally meet you! This has been quite a journey for you, hasn't it?"

Immanuel: "Amen, and it's not over yet..."

Alison: "Let's hope it won't be uneventful."

Immanuel: "Where are we?"

Alison: "Benguela, Angola. There's a private airport nearby where we'll be flown into Zambia... From there it's about a four-day drive into the remote territory of the Melimbe's, depending on conditions."

Immanuel: "That is rigorous!"

Alison: "It can be at times."

Immanuel: "Forgive me for asking, but how does a woman like you survive in a terrain like this?"

Alison: "It's quite beautiful here actually, and I'm well cared for."

Immanuel: "I can see that...! So tell me about this tribe..."

Alison: "Sure... The Melimbe's are a peaceful and musical people. Spiritually they are monotheists who believe that living in kind harmony with nature is essential for survival. This belief alienates them from most of the surrounding tribes, also that they are awaiting redemption by a great man of light who will come to them before the Sun turns dark."

Immanuel: "Very interesting, but that doesn't explain why was my family killed?"

Alison: "The Zukama Marundo, a neighboring tribe was brutal to the Melimbe's. And still are! One of their practices is to kill all the parents and children giving birth to or born as twins, triplets, and so on..."

Immanuel: "That's crazy! Why?"

Alison: "Well they believe womb-sharing will result in resource and territory divisions, favoring the tribe who has had the multiple births."

Immanuel: "And they actually believe that?"

Alison: "Yes and they fiercely enforce it! The night they invaded your parents' village, baby Emily was asleep. You got up and wandered away on your own. It was rumored that you were banging on a tree stump, making music, and prophesying to warn the others of an imminent attack. You got lost trying to find your way back. During that time..., your family was killed and the village was burned."

Immanuel: "Oh, God!"

He shouts out, grabs his ears, and bends over putting his head between his knees, while breaking out into a sweat, trembling uncontrollably.

Alison: "Goodness, Jesse, what happened? Are you having some type of seizure?"

Immanuel sits up and starts coughing, gasping for air. Alison stops the jeep and offers him water.

Alison: "Here..., drink something."

Immanuel: "Uh..., I remember this. I can still smell the smoke and hear the people screaming..."

Alison: "I'm so sorry! Perhaps I shouldn't have told you."

Immanuel: "I've never felt so hopeless, empty, and angry in my life! Take me to the airport..., I don't need to go any further... I've got the picture."

Alison: "I'm very sorry about your family, Jesse. But if this is any consolation..., the Melimbe's adored your parents. They were treated like royalty because they healed, protected, and educated the tribe. And there is more to your story... can we finish our mission together?"

Immanuel, feeling despondent and like he was kicked in the stomach full force, agrees to proceed.

Immanuel: "If you feel we must..., then yes."

Immanuel is silent for the rest of the journey through different terrains in Angola, until they arrive at the airport and board the small waiting plane to fly into Zambia.

Meanwhile, it is a sunny late afternoon in the City as Aimee finishes writing her letter to Immanuel and gets up to brew a cup of coffee. When she returns to her desk with it, she sits down to re-read and edit the email before sending it. She doesn't know he is out of the Country and away from all communication devices.

"Immanuel..., there were so many things I wanted to say to you, but time and circumstances did not permit it... To begin with, of course I wanted to make love with you. I love you with all my heart and desired passionately to express it all to you in the most artful ways, as lovemaking is a high art form."

She picks up her notebook and lies down on her bed with it as the coral setting sun streams in her window, beaming across her pregnant belly.

"People have no idea what sexuality really is. They treat it as a sport, as indulgence, as gluttony; or in narcissism, as entertainment or for pleasure alone. But it is so much more than that. And because I know this deeper meaning, I was unable to cheapen it by acting the way the world acts."

The phone rings and she checks to see if, by chance, it is Immanuel calling. Seeing it is Clara, she picks up briefly.

Aimee: "Hey Clara, I'm just finishing a letter. Can I call you back later?"

Clara: "Sure thing! Just checking in on Mom and babes."

Aimee: "What would I do without you? Give me an hour."

Clara: "You're on! Hey, wrote a song for the twins. Can't wait to play it to you. Call me when you finish."

Aimee disconnects and continues editing the letter.

"When you kiss someone you love on the lips, your breath mingles with his breath, your soul burns like bringing two candles together into one big flame, it burns with his flame. When your bodies lock into each other and become one, and you dance the sacred dance of life, here's what's really happening... and there's nothing casual about it. Oh, how we've been so misled and deprived in this culture..."

The phone rings again. She checks, hoping...., but this time it is Roger.

Aimee: "Hi Roger, I'm working on a letter, can I call you tonight?"

Roger: "Yes, do that. I want to tell you about my visit from a Detective Grady. Has he been by you yet?"

Aimee: "No. Should I be expecting him?"

Roger: "Hard to say. Get back to what you're doing and we'll talk later."

Aimee: "Okay. You've got me curious now. I'll catch you before ten."

Roger: "Right-O."

They both hang up and she sits and ponders Roger's call for a moment, then continues ...

"You see the man is like the priest, and the woman is like the temple. The priest is to be draped in purity and the woman is to be adorned with beauty. When the priest goes into the temple it is to worship God in a holy sanctuary. When he releases his seed, it is as if he dies in her arms, and she in his, sacrificing their old, separate lives to be renewed into the eternal oneness of their love. It is also as a sign of the union of our souls when they pass from this world into the loving arms of our Creator."

She gets up to refill her coffee cup.

"When the man goes to another woman, it is as if a priest of God has gone to worship in a foreign temple, committing adultery with a foreign god. Or if the temple of God allows a foreign priest to enter and perform his sacrifice therein, she is letting the temple be defiled by the worship of the unclean, foreign god. And that is one of the aspects, offered from a purely spiritual perspective, something nobody knows..."

"As an artist, I reiterate, it is the highest form of art when love is the guiding force within it. All mammalian life is recreated this way, and even some life that is not warm-blooded. The creation of life is an act of God entrusted to us. So the dance was made delicious, so that we would savor all its glories, the fragile and vacillating polarities between man and woman revealed as the intimate delicacies of soul".

"Now I must tell you... we are most assuredly soul mates, and I have found the proof in your DNA and mine. When I see you again, I hope it will be soon, I will show you one of the greatest wonders of the world. Sadly, someone has stolen my data, but there are police working to recover it. Immanuel, it is earth-shaking indeed. I have seen the creation of a new soul. The night I was to present it, Dalisay was killed trying to find out who had taken our research."

Sandy calls to see if she's sent the letter.

Aimee: "Oh Sandy, I am just editing the letter to Immanuel. It's so cathartic. Can I call you later?"

Sandy: "Of course. I can't wait to hear it. Go girl!"

She hangs up and turns off the phone to avoid further interruption. She reclines and edits the final paragraphs.

"Immanuel... there are some things I want to tell you about Love, and about our love ... And it is this: we know that love actually exists; it isn't only a concept, not just an illusion, nor merely a cultural indoctrination. It is a force, a feeling, an act of one's will, a relational status, a substance, and a realm. And in the spiritual sense, you can say it is the very personhood and presence of God."

"But how do we know? Because people are moved and changed by it! It keeps things alive, and without it, they die. It makes them grow, and without it they are stunted. It is the most inspiring force on earth – the desire to love and be loved. It is a nutrient for the heart and every other part of a living being."

"Everything that lives responds to love, seeks it, and rejoices when in union with it. Once created, it never dies or fails in its mission when true. Though it may go into a sleep state or be transposed into another form, love can always be reawakened, as the Spring."

"Love speaks in private languages, expresses itself in poetic mysteries, and brings forth the best of all things for those who seek, find, and cultivate it. As a fiery breath it combusts within a person and grows from that explosion: a living body of love, an essence, a mist, or flame that cannot dwell alone as it sings, dances, rejoices and continues to generate new life into which it deposits itself. Love is the seed and glue of life! And I miss you so very much. Without your love I feel like I'm coming undone..."

"But I must tell you about the soul now, for I have discovered the truth concerning it, and within me are growing two new, living souls. Immanuel, I am pregnant with your twins, a boy and a girl."

"My love, my mate, my joy, I've discovered the fourteen aspects of the living soul in unique ways never before addressed in research or even in theory. These are the questions I have answered and cannot wait to present to the world, and especially, to you. So here is the summary of my research. If anything happens to me, please proceed with it accordingly. I know you had many questions which I could not address when we were together, as I was overcome with my feelings for you. I hope this helps in your search for yourself. It has helped me, and I hope it will illume many others when it goes public.

"Does the soul exist? Yes it does, it is real not just a concept, myth, or imagination.

"What is it? What is it made of? It begins when a sperm meets an egg and penetrates the cell wall. An explosion of life takes place as it bursts in. It begins as a vibration, which we found was a unique song to every individual, then through a process like sonoluminescence, it turns into a fire body of light, the ideal inner lining of the physical being it inhabits. And as light, gravity does not hold it the same.

"Where does it come from? It is a product of the two parents and their entire ancestral lineage back to the first man and woman. In their DNA are coded all the deeds of their lives, and the DNA produces the soul of the person, the code of their identity.

"Does it pre-exist and at some point enter the physical person? No, it does not. It is created at the instant the person is conceived as an inseparable, until death, animated self.

"Can it travel from an animal into a person or another animal? No, each one is unique to the body it dwells within, entirely tied to that individual.

"Where does it go after life? I have not yet answered this, Immanuel, but I now know it to be the immortal image and essence of the person that once it is created, it never ceases to exist. I also believe in heaven, especially because I have felt it in your arms, and it is a promise for the resting place of love.

"Is every soul unique and different? Yes, it is more individualized even than one's fingerprints. It is a song that tells the whole story of your life and how it fits into context with everything else.

"Please forgive me, my love, I'll have to cut down the remaining answers. I'm starting to feel some abdominal pain and am finding it hard to continue.

"Are souls also male and female like bodies? Yes. they are, distinctly and permanently so.

"Do animals also have souls? They definitely do, like humans, though as the bodies of creatures differ, so do souls match the bodies they animate.

"Are the arts, poetry, dance, and music: soul languages? Most assuredly, they are, but I cannot explain this scientifically yet. Perhaps next year.

"Does each soul have a unique purpose and a personal destiny? Yes, because individuals are all like pieces of a grand puzzle filling a spot that only they are formed to fill. I know you will find yours and that right now it is the most important thing to you.

"How does the soul differ from the person? It is remote from the physical world, but is the true person inside the body. You can see when someone dies only their body remains, and is called such. It is obvious that the person himself is no longer there. These things are hard to put into words, Immanuel, but the soul is the actual person, and is the part of the person that actually feels the full spectrum of our emotions. The body and soul sync as one, and each interacts seamlessly with the other to facilitate the vibrancy of life, love, and inspiration. The soul can die while the body still lives, and a living soul can suffer in a dying body. Yet they cannot exist apart in this world, though they're sometimes incompatible.

"Does each person have only one soul mate? It is unlikely that a person can have more than one due to the genetic alignments that exist between them as well as the cultural influences on their lives. What

I have felt with you is unlike anything I've ever felt before. It's much deeper, more intimate and personal. Please don't be afraid when I tell you these things. I say them for love, not to put you in debt to me.

"How can you know who your soul mate is? Yes, I have found this scientifically, and I can't wait to show you. But I'd also have to say it's been known for centuries before science, as something you feel, that rare and magnificent match that if a person is fortunate, comes once in a lifetime, then lasts forever. If not here, at least, there...

"I know we never talked about my personal beliefs and how it interplays with my research, but I just wanted you to know who I really am apart from whatever impression you may have gotten. I hope with all my heart that they don't turn you off. If you disagree, I still love you just the same. You are to me all that I've said. I'll write again after the children are born and send some pictures. Good night for now.

Aimee clicks on send, starts to cry, then gets a very strong labor pain. Her water breaks so she calls Clara right away to get an ambulance and come to the hospital with her. She endures labor for seven hours until she gives birth to her twins: Jessica and Michael who are healthy and about seven pounds each. Clara stays by her side through the night, sleeping in the adjacent bed.

Twenty Four

Immanuel and Alison have safely landed in Zambia where they are picked up in a jeep by the Melimben Anthropologist, Dr. Gregory Hunswebo.

Alison: "Hello, Dr. Hunswebo..., this is Jesse McFarland."

Gregory: "Oh, I am so very blessed, you are amazing to behold! And standing before me! I can't believe it!"

Alison: "Gregory Hunswebo is a Melimben. He personally knows every member of the tribe, and has access to the most remote regions where they dwell."

Gregory: "Ha..., oh yes..., and they know me too! We play music together..."

Immanuel: "Really? They have instruments?"

Gregory: "Of course..., we make our own! All kinds..."

The three of them ride off through the desert, then they proceed into the jungle toward the territory of the Melimbe's. African animals and insects pass them as they go. Giraffes grazing on tree tops, zebras running wild, and the sighting of an Elephant clan in the distance as they drive on. Immanuel's amazed at the diversity of life and the beauty of all the animals he sees there despite the inherent hardships of the climate and conditions.

Immanuel: "What kinds of songs do the Melimbe people sing?"

Gregory: "Oh yes, they make their own songs. When a woman becomes pregnant, all the people will bring the new mother into the center of the village. Then they will gather around her and sing, until one woman is inspired by the Spirit to sing the song of that child in the womb. It is a new song only for him. Nobody else can have this same song."

Alison: "I've seen this done. It is amazing to observe..."

Gregory: "Yes..., and when the child is born they will also sing it. They will sing the song again on important days, and even if he does something bad, to remind him of who he is, so he cannot get lost in life and forget his purpose."

Immanuel: "This must be where my strange talent comes from... I was born here among this tribe, so I must have a soul song too. That's what I have to know. How can I find my song?"

Gregory: "That is why you are here. We are going to find your song. There is only one old woman who knows it. She is the one who received it on the day of your standing before the people of the village."

Immanuel: "Do you know how to find her?"

Gregory: "Yes, we are going there now. She has been waiting for your return for more than forty years. But she is very sick now."

Immanuel: "Waiting for me? Why?"

Gregory responds with a big smile and gentle, deep laugh...

Gregory: "Oh..., it is your song!"

Back in the City, it is a hot, humid work day as Detective Grady revisits Roger for some additional information.

Grady: "We're investigating a report of him leaving the Country, as you had mentioned. He was scheduled on a flight to Zambia, but never boarded the plane."

Roger: "Doesn't surprise me. He's cagy."

Grady: "Any idea where he may be? Or why he never made it to the airport?"

Robert: "Not a clue!"

Gregory, Alison, and Immanuel search for the elder tribeswoman by going from hut to hut; they ask all who might know of her whereabouts. Because of the importance of the knowledge she carries, her life has always been in danger of the Marundos.

After several days, they come upon a small group of huts, where one village woman alone knows and guards the elder tribeswoman who knows the song. At first she is very secretive and evasive with the team, until Gregory explains who Jesse is. As he informs her, her eyes open wide with recognition, so she agrees to take them to the woman.

She tells her family she's going to show the strangers the hidden jungle where the tribeswoman is being cared for. Then they go to the area together.

When they come upon her hut, the village woman goes in to check her first. The tribeswoman is the oldest Melimben in the village, now diabetic and blind, she was the one who was inspired and received the soul song of Jesse. This has great meaning to her for several reasons.

First, Immanuel's parents saved her and the Melimbe tribe from a deathly illness that was wiping out the entire village around the time of Immanuel's birth. Second, because of who Immanuel is believed to be, and what he will do for them and for the world.

One of her beliefs was that when she sang his song, she would regain her sight and be the first of the tribe to see him. By this she would know it was really him.

Gregory takes them in, introduces Jesse in her native tongue, the woman becomes excited and starts to cry. But she debates whether or not it is really him. When she is convinced, she reaches out to touch his hands and feel his face. She can tell from his features that he is like his parents. Then she begins trying to remember his song. She struggles through it roughly, but then gains momentum and remembers it clearly. After she sings it, she begins to tremble as her vision is restored. She sees him and reaches out to hug Jesse.

She repeats in her language: "Thank God, you have come back to your people. You have come to bring the promise. And you have given me back my eyes."

Immanuel: "Please don't give me credit for that, I didn't do anything. But that song..., what does it mean? Do you know?"

Gregory: "Yes, I can translate it for you: 'He was a little twig from the great tree, whose son will be greater than he. His father saved my life but I lost my eyes. He has come to make the darkness to see, for he is very wise. He will lead many people to the light. When I see him, I will regain my sight.'"

Immanuel: "Damn, that's my song? Are you sure? I'm feeling something weird here..."

Gregory: "There is more: 'He will raise up the poor and will lead us through the golden door. He will rescue and save, be humble and brave. He will serve the great One, and from the ways of evil he will run. See, see, see our soldier of love, for resting upon him is the spirit of the dove.'"

Immanuel: "That's it! That is my song! I felt it deep in my soul, vibrating through my whole body! I can't believe this woman adored me all these years. Her love and hope is probably what's kept me alive!"

The elder woman hugs Jesse tightly, and cries with the joy of fulfilled recognition. The woman who took them there cries with joy knowing what this will mean to the tribe.

The mission now being complete, Gregory and Alison take Jesse back to the local airport where he boards a small plane for a short flight to the airport where he can fly back to New York. He hugs and kisses them goodbye.

Jesse: "Thank you for what you've done for me. It's beyond words. I feel like a newborn! And one with a name and an identity..., oh, and a song, best of all!"

Gregory: "That is a blessing to me, as well..."

Jesse: "Please, promise me you'll take care of that woman and those people. They shouldn't have to live like that. I'll send money soon as my record deal comes through."

Jesse flies home. En route he sees an article in the newspaper explaining that Aimee's research was stolen and that Dalisay was killed. He uses Emett's phone to call Aimee but has trouble getting a call out.

When he arrives back in New York, he rents a car at the Airport. On the way into the City, he calls Aimee again and gets through.

Aimee: "Hello?"

Jesse: "Aimee..., It's me..., Jesse McFarland. I'm home... from Africa! I got it..., my soul song. Hey Mama, I know who I am now, who my parents were... I love you, you're my soul mate. I'm ready to do it... make you mine!"

She hangs up on him, hurt and wondering why he never responded to her emails, the birth of their children, and her phone messages. She doesn't know what he has been through or where he was. At first he thinks it was a dropped call, so he tries several times, but gets a busy signal, then tries one more time and gets through.

Jesse: "Baby, don't hang up, it's me. For real! Listen, I read about your Lab assistant and stolen research. Look, I'm really sorry about..."

Click, she hangs up again. He looks at the phone and murmurs aloud, turning sharply to head toward her loft.

Jesse: "Sounds like I'm gonna have to do this in person. Here we go..."

Aimee is at home resting with the twins.

While he's driving to Aimee, he calls Ed.

Jesse: "Hey, Ed, my friend, it's Jesse. You know, Immanuel. I just got back from Africa where I found my soul song. Can we get back in touch with Steve? I'm ready now!"

Ed: "Immanuel? I didn't expect a call from you... Where I'm from, someone gone that long is just presumed dead!"

Jesse: "I've got it, my soul song. Can we still get that deal?"

Ed is cozy'd up in his place with a handsome young musician he's promoting and sleeping with.

Ed: "Ha-ha! You gotta be kidding! You blew that when you stormed out on Landau!"

Jesse: "Okay, but it's way different now."

Ed: "Not for me, it isn't! You disappeared for a year, totally incommunicado. I don't have anything for you now. I've moved on to some other lines of business. But thanks for thinking of me..."

Ed looks at his flirtatious boy toy and smiles. The he hangs up and goes back to their time together. He mutters aloud.

Ed: "A clown is born, ha, that's his soul song alright!"

Jesse is now getting nervous about whether or not he will be able to overcome these shut outs, or if life is going to be the same disappointment now as it has been all along. He stops for cigarettes and a beer, when Priestess Plentavo appears. In a confused state of mind, he responds in reflex and doesn't realize who he's talking to and what he's actually saying.

Plentavo: "A small price to pay to get out of prison. Stop leading me on; how 'bout it?"

Tired and distracted by worry, he mumbles.

Jesse: "Yeah, alright... but then, lay off!"

Plentavo: "Seriously? The party just began!"

Walking back to the car, he gets a phone call.

Jesse: "Hi, Diana, suppose I should've called to apologize, but I just got back from Africa..."

Diana: "I don't care; that was no way to treat a friend!"

Jesse: "You're right... It just wasn't a good time for me."

Diana: "Alright..., we can let it go this time. But you can make it up to me tonight. I'll cook dinner and you can tell me all about your wild safari. I'd love to hear it all... Say about 7:30?"

Jesse: "Yeah, okay. It's some story; make a great film. You'd never have to do porn again."

Diana: "Sure..., we'll talk... But I don't do porn because I have to... I do it because I want to!"

As the sun sets, Jesse goes to her place. She greets him at the door in sheer, skimpy lingerie.

Diana: "Here I am... big boys toys and all! How hungry are you?"

Roger is on the way to Aimee with a couple of baby art mobiles, when he stops to do a little more surprise shopping. Meanwhile Jesse is seduced by Diana for a sex romp, and later leaves her place with messy hair, buttoning his clothing, and lighting a cigarette as he drives away.

Twenty Six

Jesse feels a little ashamed of what he just did but decides to drive by Aimee's place to look up at her apartment. He pulls up and parks across the street, watching her window with wistful sentimentality. A djembe player sits down, rhythmically prophesies at him, repeats it several times, then leaves.

Djembe Player: "The way down.., way down to Sheol is lit by the fire.., lit by the fire, it's lit by the fire in a bad man's soul..., a bad man's soul..."

Moments later a car careens out of control, and crashes into a lightpost across the street. Jesse is humored in his dreamy haze at first, as the car starts smoking.

Jesse: "Ha, I wonder if that car is old enough to smoke?"

Then he becomes concerned as flames appear. He sees the driver slumped over the wheel, so he runs to the rescue to pull him to safety.

Jesse: "Are you alright, Man? I can't get this seatbelt open?"

As he's fumbling with the seatbelt, he sees Aimee's research on the back seat, and some stuff with Robert's name imposed on it. In a glimpse he gets the whole picture.

Jesse: "Wait a minute... you're the guy I read about in the news, who stole Dr. Lucina's research. I bet you're the devil who killed Dr. Corazon too. And now I find you outside Aimee's place? I can only assume you came here to kill her too! Instead, you're gonna roast, fkn psycho! Give me that!"

Bent over the driver, half inside the car, Jesse shifts from trying to rescue him to trying to recover the research as flames begin to consume the car. There are only seconds to spare as Jesse fights for Aimee's work.

Robert: "No chance! It's mine now! And I'm going to Munich with it."

Jesse: "Munich? You delusional piece of shit! Let go! The only place you're going is to Hell in the Autobahn express lane!"

When Jesse reaches in and grabs it, he sees the "Radioactive" warning label on a container. He pauses for a moment and realizes what Robert was going to do to Aimee.

Jesse: "Radioactive? Intended for whom?"

Suddenly Robert recovers a burst of strength, grabs him, and a fight breaks out. He holds Jesse like a ghoulish zombie and handcuffs his left hand to the steering wheel. Then Robert takes out a large needle, stabs, and injects Jesse with the radioactive agent. Jesse screams and is unable to get free.

Robert: "Shine, Baby, shine!"

Just then Roger pulls up, sees the commotion, and runs over. He sees Jesse holding the research in his other hand and that he can't get free. At first he thinks that Jesse is the thief and that he's been caught and is about to receive overdue justice.

Roger: "Well now..., as fate would have it."

But then Roger looks into the car, sees the radioactive container, and that Jesse is handcuffed to the wheel. As the flames continue to spread under the hood, he realizes what's happening and runs back to his trunk to get a tool to unlock the cuffs, along with a fire extinguisher. Jesse passes the research to him.

Jesse: "Here, take this. It's Aimee's research. He's the lab ghoul who killed Dr. Corazon and was on his way to kill Aimee too."

Roger: "Hold on, I've got a monster cutter."

Jesse: "Hurry up, Man, this bomb's about to detonate!"

As Roger is running back with the cutter, the car combusts into flames. Roger sprays the car with the fire extinguisher temporarily putting out enough fire to cut off the handcuffs and pull a burnt Jesse to safety. Then he sprays Jesse to put the fire out that is burning him on the ground. He screams.

Jesse: "Aah! help, help! God, help me!"

Robert also screams for help while trying to free himself and get out of the car. Somehow he's not singed yet, the flames have strangely missed him.

Robert: "Hey, over here... what about me?"

With another burst of strength, Robert frees himself and is ready to flee his dilemma. He gloats for a second watching Roger extinguish Jesse and roll him away like a charred log. But as Robert opens the flaming door of victory to put his heel on the melting blacktop, his infernal car explodes, incinerating him.

Roger calls all the emergency services needed and waits with an agonizing Jesse until they arrive. Jesse struggles to talk, but is in too much pain, the words won't come out. All he can utter is a warning.

Jesse: "Ra... dio... ac... tive...!"

Six days later, Jesse is in a medical bubble in the hospital. He's dying, comatose, and radioactive. Aimee comes there. She stands in the doorway and looks in dazed. She is led there by nursing staff who have told her that his prognosis is terminal.

Nurse: "There's nothing more we can do."

Physician: "Even to apply a new experimental procedure, we'd need a direct family member to sign on and approve the treatment."

Aimee: "I'm his wife! He's the father of our twins! Isn't that direct enough?"

Nurse: "He's marked single on his ER apps."

Aimee: "I don't know who filled those out; I wasn't there. They obviously didn't know. See, look, these are our children..."

She shows the doctor and nurse photos of the twins, Jessica and Michael, on her phone.

Physician: "Alright. Let me know if you want to proceed with this protocol. I'll need to discuss some of the possible side effects with you. Oh, and what insurance you have. It may not cover treatment. Still, I'm not optimistic for his recovery or survival."

Nurse: "Yes, and unfortunately, I really can't let you visit with him now; hours are over at 8 pm."

Aimee: "I understand. It only takes a minute to say, 'I love you.'"

Nurse: "Okay, I have rounds across the hall, but when I come back you'll have to leave. We have to be strict about that rule; we're understaffed and if people are hanging around after visiting hours, it obstructs our patient care."

Aimee: "No problem here."

Aimee goes into his room and closes the door.

Aimee: "Immanuel..., it's me..., Aimee. Guess what? We're married now, and you have twins, a boy and a girl. In your absence I gave them my favorite names: Jessica and Michael. I forgive you for not responding to my messages and emails. I just wanted you to know how much I love you, which I can say now in this song I wrote for you..., and for us..."

Trying to focus on the positive force of her love rather than being consumed by the tragedy of his condition, she sings Jesse the beautiful love song she wrote about them, and about their children. She taped the music on a hand-held digital recorder and sings the lyrics to him live. **"Flowers On The Branch."**

After the song, Aimee collapses into the chair crying because of his suffering and imminent death. The nurse returns and peeks in, seeing her still there.

Nurse: "Leave now, please! You're interfering with our shift and jeopardizing our patients."

Aimee gathers her composure and leaves, blowing a kiss goodbye. The nurse hears the beeper go off in another room signaling patient distress, so she leaves Jesse's room to run there.

During the night when he is alone, a strong beam of light comes upon Jesse, through the ceiling, energizing and awakening him from the coma. Jesse regains consciousness and sits up as the sun rises.

The morning nurse walks in to check on him and is startled to find him awake. He's all wrapped up like a mummy but has permanently lost the use of his right hand and eye. Also his face, neck, and chest are twisted and scarred from the third degree burns, making him unrecognizable and frightening. He can no longer sing or speak because he's lost his voice. Yet, by interventions beyond the norm, some weeks after, he is released from the hospital to pursue his life's purpose despite his disfigurement and wounds.

Seven years later, Aimee is shopping around with her children, taking them out for their birthdays. They are playing music on plastic flutes as they walk. Around the corner they meet up with Clara, and give her the fourth plastic flute so she can play with them.

Clara: "Sorry I'm late for the party. And look at this! Aren't we all grown up now, seven years old, the season of reason and treason..."

Meanwhile Jesse is walking through a subway tunnel with a very large speaker strapped on his back. Thinking it could be a bomb, a commuter runs to find the police. When they see Jesse, they follow him while communicating with each other at various points, to summon a league of law enforcement, including K-9 units, and national guardsmen.

As he approaches the stairs, they close in on him as a possible terror suspect. Seeing them coming he starts to run, barely able, but makes it to the top of the steps with the cops chasing him. As soon as he gets up onto the street, he struggles to turn on the music that will play through the speaker. The cops hear it and stand back realizing he's not strapped to an explosive device. And something about the music redirects their call to pursuit.

It is a hauntingly beautiful song. First one cop hears it and follows him. Then another officer hears and follows. A passerby turns his head to listen as Jesse passes, then pivots and follows him. One after another, strangers on the street, all kinds of people from every highway of life, when they hear the song, without a word spoken, they turn and follow Jesse.

A military helicopter records the video of these last few minutes of this journey. As a blazing red setting sun, like a giant valentine, dips over the Hudson River, Jesse turns west and heads toward it.

Following him down this crimson canyon is a growing crowd so lengthy and dense it appears like over a million people. Some are shooting video on their cellphones, and several television news trucks are following the event. Still photos are flashing like a light show, while reporters mingle around trying to interview followers who will not be distracted.

As soon as Jesse rounds the corner he is met by his family and Clara. While they watch him pass, Jessica and Michael shout out and wave excitedly.

Jessica and *Michael:* "Hi Daddy."

Aimee also shouts out.

Aimee: "Yeah, big love with hugs and kisses from the happy face team, Daddy! Love you forever! Rock on!"

Then they also get in line to follow along with everyone else as a huge crowd forms behind Jesse, the largest ever assembled in any city, all mesmerized by the mysterious song on a perpetual loop.

When Jesse reaches the water, with the whole crowd behind him, he turns to face them, and stands there a moment, putting his head down in humility, as in a state of meditative thanksgiving and recognition. Silence falls upon the crowd as only the song echoes through the urban canyon. Anticipation rivets them.

When his peace is made, in preparation for the gift, he raises his head to the clouds along with his arms, and sings along with the song.

What is the song? It is this: the saga of every living soul from generation to generation, from time to eternity, heart to mind, and soul to spirit, from hand to hand, passed like a baton, and contained within the majestic masterwork of God's own soul song.

This is the one which sung the cosmos into existence; the same song that is expressed uniquely through each soul that contains the breath of life, as each player carries it through time from beginning to end. It is the grandest of love songs, a symphony into which every individual song fits like a puzzle piece, an integral movement in a complete composition.

When a certain verse pertaining to Jesse cycles around, the one that includes his soul song, though he was mute and unable to speak a word for seven years, he spontaneously sings along with very great passion.

As Jesse sings, he's gradually translated into a blazing column of brilliant light. The people watch in awe as its light sprinkles their heads like a baptism of fire; each being illuminated as a candle. As every soul is ignited, and the crowd is crowned with its radiance, the pillar of fire with Jesse inside dematerializes from the ground upward, then disappears with a flash, like lightning running home through the clouds.

For further information about this Book including summaries, synopses, explanations, press info, author schedules, reviews, etc., and to follow the progress of this story: Email: seviregis@msn.com

Also feel free to contact our office to receive information about other Books, Music, and Art by this author, as well as speaking engagements and other events on a variety of interesting topics.

The proceeds from our Book sales go to carry on the vision of CGGS and its various non-profit, spiritual, artistic, humanitarian, environmental, and humane activities.